"Wow." Vicky took mimosa. "I mean…wow. A the time since I left campus old."

H.P. sighed. "It's been an improbably action-packed couple of years for this middle-aged, midlist writer."

"To be fair," said Weston, "you've done a lot of boring stuff too. I'd characterize your life of late as a broad canvas of ennui stippled by pockets of intense terror here and there."

"So what's your take on everything we've told you?" asked Becky. "Do you think there's a story there?"

"I'd say there's at least five," Vicky answered. "But as obsessed as my network is with conspiracy theories, they're even more fanatical about facts. I don't suppose the authorities would be willing to corroborate your accounts?"

Weston shook his head. "Aside from Slim, I think the police would be at pains not to confirm what we've told you…at least not until they've concluded their inquiry, which could drag on for years."

"I'm afraid the only substantiative evidence we have of the tales we've recounted are the charred remains of a radio telescope, a ranch house, and a dilapidated barn," added H.P.

Jackassignation: Too Clever by Half

by

Wesley Payton

The Downstate Illinois Series

Jackassignation: Too Clever by Half

Cover Art by *The Wild Rose Press, Inc.*

The Wild Rose Press, Inc.
PO Box 708
Adams Basin, NY 14410-0708
Visit us at www.thewildrosepress.com

Publishing History
First Edition, 2024
Trade Paperback ISBN 978-1-5092-5316-6
Digital ISBN 978-1-5092-5317-3

The Downstate Illinois Series
Published in the United States of America

Dedication

For Ryan, David, and Jason—my friends from the old neighborhood—it was great growing up with you guys.

Other Wild Rose Press Titles by Wesley Payton:

Downstate Illinois
Immurdered: Some Time to Kill
Dissimiles: More's the Pity
Namastab: Transition into Decompose

Chapter 1

Weston made eyes at the blonde sitting across the way at the hotel bar. She responded by rolling her eyes, but he only grinned in return. He asked the bartender what the lady was drinking and bought her another Pimm's Royal Cup. She smiled coyly at Weston when the barman set the drink in front of her and pointed in his direction. He winked and nodded, to which she rolled her eyes once more.

I remember being better at this. He considered borrowing the barkeeper's muddler to perform an off-color magic trick to win the woman's attention, but the lighting wasn't quite right, so instead he got off his barstool, strode to the jukebox, and played a song he felt certain would arouse the lady's interest. Returning to his stool, he was pleased to find the woman moving her shoulders to the rhythm of the music. He mouthed the words: Do you want to dance? She demurely shook her head.

H.P. entered the barroom from the hotel's lobby. Weston espied him in the mirror behind the bottles of top-shelf spirits and pivoted on his stool to greet him. "What are you doing in this college town's finest hotel? Or as it'd be called in any city not surrounded by cows and corn, the Middling Inn. Isn't this place a bit above a creative writing instructor's pay grade?"

H.P. reluctantly sat on the open stool next to

Weston's. "I'm meeting my publisher here to discuss my latest Pirate Hunter manuscript."

"He drove all the way down from Chicago to meet with you in person," Weston replied. "Yikes—must be bad news."

The barkeeper approached. "What can I get you?"

"I'll have an Old Fashioned," answered H.P.

"I couldn't come up with a more fitting drink for you if I tried." Weston turned to the bartender. "Put that one on my tab. I'm always glad to stand a drink for a civil servant."

"You're not planning to stay here long, are you?" H.P. asked.

"That depends." Weston looked around vaguely.

"Was that Becky across the bar in a blonde wig? She got up and left when she spotted me come in."

"You do tend to have that effect on women. Becca enjoys a dress-up assignation now and then—you know how women tend to get in the springtime…well, maybe you don't."

The bartender returned, setting an Old Fashioned in front of H.P. and sliding a room key to Weston. "The lady left this for you—told me to tell you that she'd be in the Honeymoon suite."

Weston took the key. "I thought we reserved the Presidential suite."

"It's the same room," said the barkeeper, "top floor—first door to the left past the ice machine."

"Well hocus-pocus, I'd enjoy nothing less than to stay and drink with you, but booty calls." Weston stood from his stool. "Give my regards to that old bag of bones publisher of yours."

H.P. turned to watch as Weston exited the bar. Then

he nodded to a young woman reading a newspaper in the lobby.

The woman tucked the paper under her arm as she entered the barroom. "Is this seat taken, mister?" She kissed H.P.

"It's good to see you again, Vicky."

Chapter 2

H.P. held Vicky in bed as he watched the early morning light intensify through the hotel room's diaphanous drapes.

Vicky awoke when the stretching rays of sunlight reached her eyes. "I thought you closed the curtains last night."

"The inner ones…not the blackout curtains. I wanted to see the starlight last night after…you know."

"Yes, I remember. From what I understand, most guys usually want to watch Sportscenter postcoital—not twinkling stars."

"Is that what the handsome news anchor on your network likes to watch?"

"I was wondering when we were going to get to this." Vicky sat up. "Convenient that you didn't broach the subject until after we had sex."

"Listen, it's none of my business."

"No, it isn't." Vicky got out of bed, taking the top sheet with her. "But if you want to know the truth—"

"I'm not sure that I do," H.P. interrupted, pulling up the comforter from the foot of the bed.

"Guess what—you're going to hear it anyway. All that on-air byplay is just for ratings. Sure, we've had dinner a couple of times, but we've never done this. From what I've been told, he's got a revolving door on his bedroom, and I don't care to be the umpteenth customer of the month. Besides, he's better looking, wealthier, and more famous than you…as well as considerably younger, so riddle me this: if I were with him, then why would I be here with you?"

"I can only assume it's due to my aptitude for lovemaking."

"Wrong answer. I'm going to go take a shower—feel free not to be here when I come out."

H.P. grabbed the end of the sheet, pulling her back toward the bed. "I missed you too…and besides a brief fling earlier this year, I haven't been seeing anyone else either."

Vicky hesitantly curled up next to him. "I didn't say that exactly. I've been spending time outside of work with one of my producers. She's snarky—you'd like her."

"Ah, giving the old college try another try."

"I don't know…I didn't intend for anything to happen, but we connected."

"You mean aside from the fact that your parts don't actually interconnect."

"I meant our personalities."

"Sure, that's important too, I guess." H.P. wrapped his arms around her. "So what's this?"

"This is me being in town for a story and wanting to check in on an old friend."

"You didn't have to use that adjective."

"Former friend, then?"

"I take it back…I prefer 'old' to 'former.' I've never had a tryst with a celebrity before. What's the protocol? Should we have breakfast in that restaurant off the lobby, or should I exit alone via the service elevator?"

"I'm only a minor celebrity for people who watch

too much cable news, so a frittata downstairs for brunch sounds like a lovely idea."

H.P. checked the alarm clock on the nightstand. "It's only eight thirty…still breakfast time."

"Checkout's not until ten, and I think we ought to take full advantage of the room while we have it."

Chapter 3

H.P. and Vicky entered the small restaurant. He held the door open with one hand while dragging her wheeled suitcase with his other. Weston waved wildly from a table for four near the hostess' station. "You should come join us."

H.P. pretended not to hear Weston's invitation and didn't acknowledge his presence as he quickly scanned the rest of the restaurant. Seeing no empty tables, he preemptively asked the approaching hostess, "How long is the wait?"

"Most everyone was just seated—maybe half an hour, though we're offering a bottomless mimosa special, so…"

"Weston, is that you?" H.P. asked as he feebly feigned surprise. "I didn't notice you at first. I assumed the man waving his arm in the air like a lunatic was simply someone in urgent need of the Heimlich maneuver."

"Gosh, I'd swear your old publisher has gotten younger since the last time I saw him…and changed genders too. What plastic surgeons can do these days is just amazing."

H.P. reluctantly took a few steps toward Weston's and Becky's table. "This is my friend Vicky Donato. She's a journalist in town doing a story on…oh, we never really got around to discussing what your piece is about."

"More pressing matters came up, I'm sure," said Weston. "It's a pleasure to make your acquaintance, and despite being wholly uninformed about it, I have no doubt that H.P. has a keen interest in your piece. Allow me to introduce my wife, Becca."

"Nice to meet you," said Vicky.

"I see you're a brunette again," added H.P.

"I'm certain that I have no idea to what you're referring," Becky replied from behind a cup of coffee.

"Why don't you two dine with us?" asked Weston. "We only just sat down."

"So the hostess mentioned." H.P. pulled out a chair for Vicky and then took a seat for himself.

Weston smiled. "Always the perfect gentleman. I imagine last night—through a stroke of serendipity—that after talking with your publisher for an hour or two, you left the bar and bumped into your friend, Ms. Donato, in the lobby as she was returning to her hotel room at the end of an exhausting and exhaustive day of research for her story. Naturally, the two of you returned to the bar to have a drink and catch up on old times, but between that drink and the few you'd had previously with—what's his name…Morty—you thought better of driving home, so you inquired at the front desk about getting a room of your own, but to your dismay there were no vacancies; however, Ms. Donato very thoughtfully suggested that you sleep on her room's pullout couch, and you both slumbered chastely through the night."

H.P. nodded. "I couldn't have described the events of yesterday evening better myself."

Weston turned to Becky. "See, I told you I'm a better fiction writer than him."

"Were I you, I wouldn't be too pleased with myself," said Vicky. "Back in college, I appreciated all the little details in your book *Sapphic Spinster*, but for this story you got nearly every detail wrong—not the least of which is my name; it's Dr. Donato...not Ms."

"Ah, a learned woman," Weston replied. "I wouldn't have figured you'd be attracted to such a dullard, but then I suppose there's no accounting for taste."

Becky placed her hand on her husband's. "No, there certainly isn't."

"H.P., color me impressed," Weston continued. "You spend your professional life rubbing elbows with Ph.Ds., then come to find out you spend your personal life rubbing other body parts with them as well. A lesser man might resent being bettered at every turn."

H.P. grinned. "If ever I'm in need of a lesser man for whom I have no concern of being my better, I can always count on you."

"They'd be content to go on like this for hours," Becky said to Vicky, "but I want to hear about this story you're working on."

"Thanks...I don't know if you've been following it in the news, but since the first of the year there's been a steady flow of information coming to light about some sort of chemistry cabal that involves a number of senior executives at various biotech and pharmaceutical companies across the country. There's been several minor stories, but the prevailing thinking is—at least at my conspiracy-obsessed network—that the major story that ties each of these execs together has yet to be broken...or it could all be a red herring, and this conjecture about cabals and such is just fake news to cover up a quotidian, albeit complex, embezzlement scheme. Anyway, I got voluntold—since I was once a professor here, though my tenure was too brief to get tenured—to visit the campus and follow up on a few leads, since some of the companies have tangential ties to the university."

Weston, Becky, and H.P. looked at one another in stunned silence. H.P. spoke first. "Vicky, did your research happen to turn up anything of interest?"

"Not really...I asked a lot of questions, but as usual the people who didn't have any answers were the ones doing most of the talking—pretty much par for the course with these types of high-intrigue stories. I did hear the names Edwin and Kate Hubert on more than one occasion, so I did a little investigating, but just my luck I discovered that the newlyweds recently left for a month-long honeymoon and won't be back until next week, though I find it somewhat peculiar that Kate was recently unemployed and Edwin—despite being in his fifties—seems never to have held a permanent job, which begs the question: who's bankrolling their equatorial excursion?"

"As I understand it," replied Becky, "their all-expenses-paid trip was a signing bonus of sorts for Kate, who started as president of [company name redacted] right after they got married at the beginning of the year, thus delaying their honeymoon by a few months."

"Kate and Ed are friends of ours," added Weston. "We were all part of their bridal party."

H.P. tugged on his earlobe. "I guess we didn't catch up quite as much as we should have."

"It can be difficult to give a full debriefing while simultaneously being debriefed." Weston sipped his mimosa.

****

"Wow." Vicky took another drink of her third mimosa. "I mean…wow. And here I thought you'd spent the time since I left campus just doing the same old same old."

H.P. sighed. "It's been an improbably action-packed couple of years for this middle-aged, midlist writer."

"To be fair," said Weston, "you've done a lot of boring stuff too. I'd characterize your life of late as a broad canvas of ennui stippled by pockets of intense terror here and there."

"So what's your take on everything we've told you?" asked Becky. "Do you think there's a story there?"

"I'd say there's at least five," Vicky answered. "But as obsessed as my network is with conspiracy theories, they're even more fanatical about facts. I don't suppose the authorities would be willing to corroborate your accounts?"

Weston shook his head. "Aside from Slim, I think the police would be at pains not to confirm what we've told you…at least not until they've concluded their inquiry, which could drag on for years."

"I'm afraid the only substantiative evidence we have of the tales we've recounted are the charred remains of a radio telescope, a ranch house, and a dilapidated barn," added H.P.

"I've seen good stories rise from the ashes of bad situations before, but it'll take some elbow grease." Vicky closed her notebook. "Let me do some more poking around."

"If you need a partner to help with the poking, I'm sure H.P. would be glad to oblige." Weston grinned.

"He's especially fond of undercover work."

Vicky clicked her pen. "Congratulations...you scored two double entendres that time."

"What woman doesn't want a husband who makes her proud?" Becky asked rhetorically. "But seriously, do let us know if you turn up anything. Even though it's been months since the members of this evil chemistry committee—or whatever it was—were exposed, I still don't feel like we're out of the woods yet."

"You worry too much, Becca." Weston ran his index finger across his wife's wrist. "Slim assured us that the feds have every person listed in that dossier the cops found, who hasn't already been incarcerated, under surveillance."

"Okay," said Becky, "but what about any unlisted persons?"

Chapter 4

The association coordinator sat in his unassuming office, studying the screen of his desktop computer. He thought the résumé of the candidate he was scheduled to meet next adequate but uninspiring. He pressed the intercom button on his phone. "Send him in."

The lock of his security door buzzed. A straight up and down soldier in civilian clothes entered the office and stood at attention. The coordinator motioned to the empty chair across the desk. "Please, have a seat."

"Thank you, sir."

The coordinator eyed the young man. "At ease, son—I'm not your commanding officer, and despite most of our associates being ex-military, we try our best to blend in."

"I understand." The young man relaxed his shoulders.

"I've been reviewing your résumé one of your comrades emailed me. As he must've mentioned, he's done some work for this association in the past. Anyway, he speaks very highly of you, and as a courtesy to him I agreed to meet with you. Your credentials are quite impressive—U.S. Coast Guard Maritime Security Response Team specializing in VBSS operations...all the counterterrorism action you boys see puts you on par with the Navy SEALs in my book."

"Begging your pardon, sir, but MSRTs are like orcas

compared to SEALs."

The coordinator grinned. "I like your spirit, son, but the reality is that you're a blunt instrument...a badass one to be sure; however, our association is looking more for scalpels—operatives who're surgical and can get in close to make small incisions—not bash 'em over the head types who leave behind big bruises, but I'll keep your résumé on file, and we'll be in touch if any contracts requiring your qualifications come our way."

The young man frowned. "I think there's been a misunderstanding, sir. I'm not here looking for a job. I came here with a job in mind."

"Most irregular." The coordinator leaned back in his chair. "You've got my attention, son...what sort of job?"

"It has to do with my grandad who was also a guardsman back in the day—long before the MSRTs or even the Deployable Operations Group, but still...he was not a man to be trifled with."

"I have no doubt of it...so what happened to him?"

"After serving a long and distinguished career in the Guard, during which he survived many close calls, he ultimately became a barfly and a bum...eventually succumbing to his alcoholism."

The coordinator interwove his fingers behind his head. "Son, I'm truly sorry to hear that...but, as I'm sure you're aware, not all wounds are visible and—despite conventional wisdom—not all of them heal in time."

"I know that, but after such an honorable record of service, he deserved a better fate. I need your help to set things right, and—as it happens—I think I'm in a position to help you in the process."

"If your beef is with the Coast Guard, I'm not sure how I can be of any help at all. I've met many soldiers over the years who've been mistreated in one way or another during their time in the military, but—"

"You don't understand." The young man shook his head. "My quarrel is not with the military, but with the man who stole my grandad's legacy…the story of his time as a guardsman. You see, back in his heyday Grandpa was known as the Pirate Hunter, and years later the man who plied him with the booze that took his life is the same man who coopted his life's story as a work of fiction. I believe this writer—who's made a career out of exploiting my grandad's exploits—is known to you as well, and I think it's about time for us both to settle the score."

The coordinator leaned forward and placed his elbows on the desk. "Pretend for a moment that I don't have any idea who you're talking about…just what is it that you're proposing?"

"I have it on good authority that you've sworn off taking any more direct action against H.P. and his cohort. Word around the campfire is that your association has lost several operatives while trying to snuff them, and you're concerned that any further attempts would draw unwanted attention to your organization. But what if it wasn't you making the play?" The young man cocked his head to the side. "Tell me, how long do you think it'll take for the authorities to arrest and interrogate all those people listed in that dossier I keep hearing about? Don't you think that eventually the feds will connect their stories about the associates they paid to do their dirty work to the stories H.P. and his group have been telling about the boogeymen they've been beset by? What if I could guarantee you—with the backing of your association resources—that I could finally take down

H.P. and his group?"

The coordinator glanced again at his computer screen, rereading the name at the top of the résumé. "How do you pronounce your surname…like *lead*, as in the soft metal?"

"No…as in *lead*, follow, or get out of the way."

Chapter 5

Weston drove Becky's Jeep into the parking lot of Vance's residence hall as she called to inform him of their arrival. "Vancy's not answering."

"It's past noon." Weston pulled into a spot near the rear entrance of the tall building. "Van doesn't usually sleep through lunchtime."

"Should we go up unannounced?"

"You texted him yesterday that we'd stop by today in the early afternoon—to my mind that qualifies as an announcement."

"He did text back to say he'd be in." Becky looked up at the dormitory through the windshield. "Maybe his cellphone needs charging."

****

Becky and Weston stepped off the elevator onto Vance's floor and walked down the corridor to his dorm room. They found his door ajar but no one within.

"Maybe he's still at lunch," said Becky.

"I believe the cafeteria closed a half hour ago."

A lanky freshman with a less than fulsome beard stopped in the doorway. "Are you two looking for Van the Man?"

"We are indeed," answered Weston.

"I saw him in the restroom like ten minutes ago." The freshman flashed a peace sign and continued on down the hall.

"You wait here," Weston said. "I'll go check to see if he's in the washroom."

Weston entered the men's room at the end of the hallway. The two banks of sinks were unoccupied, and no water was running in the showers, so he rounded the corner to the row of toilets and noticed only one pair of feet under the stalls, though the soles were facing up rather than flat on the floor. He recognized the sneakers. As he approached the stall, he heard the sound of retching. "Van, is that you?"

"Who's asking?"

"Jesus, Van, I'm not a damn bill collector. It's me…you know, your mother's husband."

"Oh…hey, Weston…sorry, I'm a little indisposed at the moment."

"Yeah, you don't sound like you feel too well."

"It's only a head cold."

"Then I suppose all that vomit I just heard came out of your brain."

Vance sighed. "Listen, I had sort of late night…or maybe more of an early morning. Anyway, I guess I overdid it a bit—beer after liquor and all."

"In my experience the order doesn't matter so much as the quantity."

"Right, that might've had something to do with it as well…could you not tell my mom?"

"Van, I think she'd understand. She went to college too. You're allowed to occasionally get drunk in your youth. It's not until you become middle aged like me when people label you a drunk."

"I get what you're getting at, but considering my dad's struggles with substance abuse…I just don't want her to worry."

Weston nodded. "That's thoughtful, Van. Sure, I'll tell her you're using the facilities in the way they were intended. We'll wait for you in your room while you get cleaned up."

"Thanks, Weston."

"You bet...by the way, the dining hall's closed for lunch now, but we brought you a half-eaten omelet leftover from our brunch, and even though the cheese is a bit runny, and the mushrooms a little slimy, it should still be quite tasty, although I hope it didn't get too soggy and sweaty in its Styrofoam container." Weston paused as Vance retched again. "There you go...get it all out—see you soon."

****

Becky hugged Vance as he entered his dorm room. "There's my Vancy boy."

"Mom, I asked you not to call me that...it sounds like you're saying Nancy boy."

Becky looked her son up and down. "Why's your hair wet?"

"Oh, I just took a quick shower."

"But you're still wearing your pajamas."

"I was planning to spend the day studying in my room...so no reason to get dressed."

Becky took a step back. "You don't smell like you just showered."

"Well...I more stuck my head in the sink and ran the faucet for a few seconds."

"Becca, what's with the third degree?" asked Weston. "Van's here now...we're all here."

Vance nodded in agreement. "Yeah...it's good to see you guys. Mom, you mentioned in your text that Lance and Ance were staying with Aunt Kim so that you two could spend the night at a hotel here. Was there like a book event in town…or did you go see a show or something?"

Becky scratched the top of her head. "No, we came here to…uh, that is we just wanted…to hear about how you're doing."

Chapter 6

H.P. sat in his attic with his feet up on the writing desk—the blank screen of his laptop mocking him. He averted his gaze by staring at the rafters. *Yep…they're still there.* He'd taken a leave of absence from his teaching position for the spring semester, believing with all the new ideas he'd had for his Pirate Hunter character that he could complete the first draft of his latest installment by the time he was due back in the fall. Instead, it was starting to feel more like he'd taken a leave of his senses. He'd written most of the manuscript in two months, and for the two months since he'd written almost nothing. Now he had four more months until he was scheduled to resume his teaching duties, but he had serious doubts about whether it would be enough time to come up with a suitable conclusion.

H.P. had decided months before to set the Pirate Hunter on an ice floe—figuratively at first, though recently in desperation he'd entertained the literal possibility as part of the denouement—since book sales in his series had been trending downward over the past several years. Then, quite by chance, he'd had—or imagined that he'd experienced—an out-of-this-world idea for a new and altogether unique episode in his Pirate Hunter saga. His sales soon increased after the book's release, and he'd thought an opportunity had presented itself to go out on top, but then Weston had proposed a collaboration—a teaming up of his Pirate Hunter and Weston's Spinster character. Again, the idea for this new installment in the Pirate Hunter's story seemed too unique to ignore; however, once he realized that he'd be doing the lion's share of the writing, he'd wished he had.

Now H.P. felt as if he was in a rut yet again. After a world-hopping adventure, followed up by an unlikely partnership, his Pirate Hunter seemed to be back in all too familiar waters. The sameness was not in what he'd written thus far, but in what awaited him—as inevitable as the tide itself: the ending. Should he kill off the Pirate Hunter once and for all? He could start a new series with different characters. He might lose half his readership, but if the new characters were interesting and the story engaging he might win twice that many first-time readers; however, if that next book turned out to be a bomb, then those nagging self-doubts—as well as the offhand remarks and passing comments he'd heard too often over recent years—would be confirmed; he wasn't a good writer, just a lucky one who decades before happened to come up with a character familiar enough but also fresh enough to find a devoted audience, though now he felt that audience's devotion waning.

The hardest part is deciding which tack would better preserve the Pirate Hunter's dignity—either letting him sail into the sunset, leaving the last leg of his journey untold, or killing him off and running the risk of no one caring.

H.P. had been cogitating in this manner for what felt like weeks on end. Little did he know that his ruminations would take a decisive turn with the envelope being delivered at that very moment.

When he heard the doorbell ring, H.P. shot up from

his desk chair like a rookie firefighter responding to a five-alarmer. He raced downstairs the way a child on Christmas morning would, eager for an interruption to his contemplations. *Perhaps Vicky decided to stay in town for another few days to continue researching her story.* However, when he reached the front door, he found no one waiting on his porch.

Instead, he saw a delivery van pulling out of his driveway. He waved to the driver as he stooped to pick up the manila envelope from his welcome mat. *Curious. No return address.* He reentered his house as he tore open the top of the envelope. Inside was a single, handwritten page. He began reading the yellowed piece of loose-leaf paper and soon recognized it as a page from his first draft of the first volume in his Pirate Hunter series that he'd written nearly three decades ago.

Chapter 7

Weston sauntered into the Boutonniere and spotted Slim sitting alone at the bar. He sat down on the stool next to his and nodded at the approaching bartender. "Two more of what he's drinking."

The bartender pulled a pair of longneck bottles from the cooler. "I remember you...don't you usually try ordering something a bit more highbrow than beer? Scotch comes to mind."

"I'm trying to cut back on my whiskey drinking these days." Weston looked around. "Kind of dead in here tonight."

The bartender pried off the beer caps with a novelty bottle opener. "Been kinda dead in here all decade, though this on-again/off-again pandemic sure ain't helped business none these past few years."

"Becky mentioned you had a bout with the virus a couple weeks back," Slim said. "Any symptoms?"

Weston shook his head. "Just some hoarseness...mostly in my pants—nothing out of the ordinary for me."

The bartender set the beers on the bar in front of his only two patrons. "I remember you real good now—wiseacre, ain't ya?"

Slim smiled. "You don't know the halfwit of it."

"Most people mistakenly believe that the word 'wiseacre' comes from the German Weisenheimer, but it's actually Dutch in origin and translates as 'soothsayer,' which is a psychic of sorts." Weston sipped his beer. "So, my good man, I take no umbrage at you calling me a wiseacre."

The bartender frowned. "Did I say you were a wiseacre? Because what I meant to call you was a wiseass."

Weston nodded. "See, I knew you were going to say that."

The bartender flicked his grimy bar rag over his linebacker shoulder and huffed off.

"You still have a knack for endangering—I mean endearing yourself with the locals," observed Slim.

"I've only lived here for a few years," said Weston. "Fitting in with the yokels is a process…you can't rush these things. So why did you want to meet up all the way out here? You should've just come by the house if you wanted to have a beer."

"I didn't want to upset Becky."

"Don't be self-conscious; I'm sure Becca's gotten used to seeing your gruesome mug by now."

"That's funny, Don Wrinkles…no, I got some news from a friend of mine on the force upstate who's helping with the investigation of the folks identified in that dossier we came across on New Year's Eve, and I know Becky's still on pins and needles about that whole business—frankly, I ain't all that at ease about it myself."

"What's to worry about? Every time a perpetrator pops up, we put them in their place and come out smelling like a rose on the other side."

"You and me got different ideas of how a rose smells." Slim took a swig of beer. "Tell me, you still driving Becky's Jeep after I had to crash your car into that barn to save you all from roasting to death?"

"I'm weighing my options…these new cars today come with too many fancy gizmos, but I don't think you want to be giving me a hard time about my vehicle situation since I haven't mentioned to Becca how I've happened to notice your truck parked in front of her sister's house on those early mornings when I drive Lance to band practice at the middle school."

"Kim and I are just friends."

"You and I are friends, but I don't stop by your place at six in the morning to shoot the breeze."

"What I wanted to tell you is more than just shooting the breeze, so listen up. As I told you before, all those people listed in that dossier—at least the ones we were able to track down—have been under surveillance…including their communications through various backchannels, and them that's doing the surveilling have noticed a pattern. Each time they discuss some goings-on that took place outside of a lab setting— and what I mean is work that necessitated guns—they mention the terms 'associates' or 'association' just like them boys out at Ed's old satellite talked about."

Weston nodded. "Right…H.P. and I also heard about the association during our ordeal out at his place."

"I don't remember you making note of that in the police report."

"It might've slipped my mind. As you may recall, it was a rather eventful day, and the exact terms that were bandied about didn't seem quite as salient as me and H.P. nearly being burned alive."

Slim rubbed his forehead. "Anyway, the prevailing theory now is that this association isn't just some small-time operation used by a couple factions of the network of pharma executives we've had under surveillance for the past few months but instead an entirely separate and potentially just as far-reaching organization that they'd partnered with—think Ford and Firestone."

"Okay."

"Okay?"

"I'm not seeing the issue. We took down—"

"The authorities are in the process of taking down," interrupted Slim.

"Ford, if you like, is being taken down as we speak, so who cares about the company that supplied their tires?"

"As you might remember, when the hundred-year Ford/Firestone partnership went south, things got ugly fast. We're squeezing the life out of what was likely this association's biggest client. You don't think there'll be ramifications? These so-called associates would have a vested interest in silencing the group that was responsible—"

"For taking them down?" Weston interrupted.

"For causing them and their client so many headaches. I wouldn't be surprised if they got a plan in the works to permanently muzzle that mouth of yours."

"Slim, you're getting worked up for no good reason. I think your Ford/Firestone analogy is apt. These are businesspeople who're all about conducting cost/benefit analyses. Where's the benefit to this association in the cost of sticking its head up from cover to take a shot at me, since I'm in no way involved with the actual investigation that's underway into their former client, which may or may not turn out to incriminate them? There's no profit in revenge."

"Maybe not, but businesspeople are still people, and when people with power get their egos bruised, they tend to react in nasty ways."

"Thanks for that bit of reductio ad absurdum, but if this association is as large as you seem to think it is, then I'm sure the last thing on their minds it little old me."

Slim set his beer on the bar. "Be that as it may—"

"Congratulations, you managed to string together five monosyllabic words in a row."

"Nevertheless, I wanted to inform you that from now on you'll be seeing a lot more patrol cars driving past your house until this matter gets cleared up to my satisfaction."

"Jesus, I ought to retire from writing and start manning a tollbooth at the end of my driveway with all the squad cars you've dispatched down my road over the last couple years."

Chapter 8

Mr. Lead sat on a couch in the outer office of the publisher he'd come to see. The publisher's secretary looked up again from her desk. "Are you sure I can't get you a bottle of water or a cup of coffee?"

Mr. Lead shook his head. "No thank you, ma'am."

"Okay…he should be able to see you soon."

Just then the door to the inner office opened. The publisher emerged with his hand extended. "Mr. Lead, sorry to keep you waiting."

Mr. Lead stood but declined the offered handshake. "It's actually pronounced *lede*, as in don't bury it."

The publisher stuck his right hand in his pocket. "Ah, well you can just call me Morty…please, step into my office."

Mr. Lead followed the publisher in and took a seat in a wingback chair as Morty sat behind his desk. "I understand you've brought a manuscript with you. I don't usually accept unsolicited queries by unagented writers, but the gentleman who just called was very persuasive…and well connected. He made it clear that I need to see what you have."

"Yes, I believe you'll find this of interest." Mr. Lead slid a stack of handwritten pages across the desk.

"I can't remember the last time I reviewed something in longhand." Morty took up the manuscript and thumbed through the first few pages. "I don't understand…this appears to be an early draft of one of my writer's debut novel."

Mr. Lead nodded. "That's exactly what it is. This is the original draft of the first Pirate Hunter book, penned by my late grandfather, who was known as the Pirate Hunter during his time in the Coast Guard. I found this manuscript last month in his footlocker, which had been sealed in a storage unit belonging to my recently deceased father for over twenty years."

Morty raised an eyebrow. "I'm sorry for your loss, young man; however, I'm not sure what I can do for you."

"You've published every book in my grandad's eponymous series, including the last one, which was co-authored by Weston Payley."

"Yes, that's correct—H.P.'s Pirate Hunter novels have been among our best sellers over the years…so what is it that you want precisely?"

"What I want, precisely, is my grandfather's cut. Grandad died penniless, while books based on his time in the service, stories stolen by a man who barely knew him, went on to sell millions."

"Well, millions might be something of an overstatement." Morty sighed. "We do okay here, but we're not exactly the biggest name in the business."

"So then I take it that you don't have the resources for a protracted legal battle over back royalties for the entire run of one of your 'best sellers.' "

Morty raised his hands. "Whoa…I thought we were having a friendly discussion here—not some litigious conversation."

"You hold in your hand half the original manuscript for the Pirate Hunter—a book written by my grandad.

That character and profits from all subsequent books based on him belong to my family."

"Listen, I understand how you feel…were I in your shoes, sitting on that side of the desk, I'd likely feel similarly." Morty closely examined the handwriting on the page he held. "However, how do you know your grandfather actually wrote this? Honestly, this looks to me like H.P.'s sloppy script. You say they knew each other way back when…well, maybe—"

"I didn't come here to engage in hypotheticals with you," Mr. Lead interrupted. "I'm sure you're aware that this is not the first time accusations of plagiarism have been leveled at your writer. Of course, no one can say for certain how this matter might play out if it goes to trial, but I've come today to offer you an alternative…a way to keep this business of ours out of the courts."

Chapter 9

Weston awoke on the couch when he heard the doorbell ring. He got up and opened the front door to find H.P. on the porch holding two cups of coffee. "I thought I might catch you taking your usual post-lunch siesta."

Weston stifled a yawn. "Just trying to get caught up on my beauty sleep."

"In that case I don't think a nap is going to cut it." H.P. stepped into the living room as he handed over a coffee. "I'd suggest a months-long hibernation instead."

"Thanks for the coffee and the kick in the crotch." Weston closed the front door. "When you emailed earlier, you mentioned there's a matter in which you're in want of some advice. I can only assume the issue is in regard to your personality, seeing how that's your most obvious deficiency. My unequivocal recommendation is that it's high time for you to finally procure one."

"And I thought driving over here was a long way to go." H.P. sat down in the living room's recliner. "Drink your coffee…you're not at your sharpest when you're drowsy."

Weston took a seat on the couch. "So why did you drive all the way over here? I enjoy our conversations, but I prefer to have them over the phone so that I'm spared the sight of you."

"I had to get out of the house. The prospect of having several quiet months to myself—especially considering all the goings on of the past year or so—was very appealing, but now I'm wondering if the university might be in need of my services for summer school."

Weston removed the lid from his paper cup and blew at the steam. "I take it the writing isn't going well."

"It was going well enough at first—gangbusters, really...but these past few weeks, not so much."

"Let me guess, you're at the end."

H.P. sipped his coffee. "Feels more like a dead end."

"Beginnings and endings are a two-headed beast. Middles are easy. Stuff happens, then more stuff happens—half the time it practically writes itself—but knowing when to start a story and when to stop it...well, that's a whole different ballgame."

"Rephrasing my problem...so very helpful. I am aware of the difficulty of beginnings and endings—what with being a creative writing instructor and all."

"So you say you've been blocked for a few weeks now."

"I wouldn't necessarily characterize it as writer's block, per se."

"Then you've been making slow but steady progress the past month or so."

H.P. took another sip of coffee. "I also wouldn't *not* characterize it as writer's block."

"If writing ultimately doesn't pan out for you, you sound as if you have the makings of a double-talking attorney."

"I sought your counsel because I assumed a writer as bankrupt of talent as you must've dealt with this sort of thing before."

"Lashing out is a symptom of desperation."

"Seeking your advice certainly feels desperate."

Finding his coffee to be sufficiently cooled, Weston finally took a long drink. "I'm always amused by dilettante writers who complain of writer's block. I can swing a baseball bat—or at least I used to be able to—but if I were to face a major league pitcher and strike out, I wouldn't complain of being in a batting slump. I think I'd have the self-awareness to know that I was simply out of my league."

"Ah, more sports parallels...and, pray tell, what exactly am I supposed to glean from your analogy?"

"That you've paid your dues...meaning when you first started out, you wrote without pay just like a ballplayer who plays for the love of the game, and in time you became good enough to get published and make some money doing what you love. You're not a dilettante. You're just slumping right now. It happens to every big leaguer—don't sweat it...you'll get through it."

H.P. sat back suddenly, as if he'd been beaned in the head by Weston's tacit compliment. "Thank you...that's actually helpful to hear."

"You bet. So what's your working title for this one?"

"The Pirate Hunter finds an antique boatswain's pipe at the scene of a crime, and it becomes an important key to the story, so I want to incorporate that somehow. Since this might be the last in the series, I'd like for the title to have some gravitas...something Hemingwayesque, such as *For Whom the Bell Tolls*."

"How about entitling it *For Whom the Whistle Whistles*?"

"I see that we've now transitioned past the point of our conversation in which you'll be of any help."

"Or maybe *For Whom the Bosun Toots*?"

H.P. pulled his vibrating cellphone from his pocket. "I really hope I have to take this." He studied the screen for a moment. "Oh, it's my publisher." He held the phone to his ear. "Hey, Morty, did you perchance mail me an old page from my first...okay, that's a surprising development...I understand, nothing personal...sure, we'll reevaluate in a few months." H.P. lowered his phone. "That was a most unwelcome call, though I suppose on the upside I no longer have to worry about writer's block. My publisher just delisted the complete Pirate Hunter series—perhaps indefinitely."

"That came out of leftfield," Weston replied. "Can you bring a suit against Morty to block the delisting?"

"Not when you have an attorney as dumb as mine. Once someone threatened to sue me for everything I had, and my lawyer said I—"

"Should take the deal," interrupted Weston. "Yes, you've told me that one before."

Chapter 10

Mr. Lead stepped into the chancellor's office. "I appreciate you agreeing to meet with me on such short notice."

The chancellor curtly gestured toward the empty chair in front of her desk. "My calendar is booked with meetings until two weeks after I'm dead, but frankly I received a rather cryptic email this morning from one of the university's more generous benefactors informing me that it was in this institution's best interests that I make time to see you today, and so here you are, Mr. Lead."

"It's actually pronounced Lead, as in—"

The chancellor held up her index finger. "I don't care how you pronounce your name. What is it that you want?"

Mr. Lead settled into the supple leather chair. "I have some concerns about one of your professors."

"So take them up with her or his department dean. I was told you were in the Coast Guard. Higher education has a certain hierarchy that I'm sure you can appreciate. I'm the fleet admiral—not a ship's captain. You have an issue with one of our sailors, then go talk to their direct report."

"Wouldn't the sailors be the students?"

"You don't have the luxury of time to get cute. I'm about one minute away from having you barred from campus, even at the risk of having to rename our new performing arts center."

Mr. Lead raised his hands. "My apologies—let me get right to it. One of your creative writing professors, who's a writer himself, has recently come under a cloud of suspicion for plagiarism."

"That's a serious allegation at an institution of higher learning."

"I assure you that I don't take this matter lightly. I've raised my concerns with his publisher, and he's decided to delist his Pirate Hunter series."

The chancellor sat back in her desk chair. "Oh, this is about H.P."

"Then you're familiar with his work?"

"I'm aware of it, but I wouldn't say that I'm familiar with it. H.P.'s initials have popped up on my radar before. I believe he's currently on administrative leave…the result, as I recall, of an incident that led to a misunderstanding with his dean concerning the terms of his contract or some such. H.P. has been here longer than I have, but candidly an author of a series of books about a character who hunts modern-day privateers never seemed to me the type of teacher best suited to educate our aspiring writers…and incidentally, he's an instructor—not a full-fledged professor."

"So I take it he's not tenured."

"That's correct, though I don't see how it's relevant. H.P. has been accused of plagiarism before…turns out a fellow writing instructor had hacked into his campus computer to access his personal drive on the university's network where he backed up his fiction pieces. This reprobate, who no longer teaches here, released excerpts from H.P.'s drafts soon after he'd written them in an effort to discredit him. So how is what you're attempting any different?"

"The difference is I have proof." Mr. Lead handed over several handwritten pages. "These were written by my grandfather. They're a draft of what would become the first Pirate Hunter book, for which my grandad was never credited or paid."

The chancellor held a page up to the light of her desk lamp as if checking for signs of forgery. "I'm not sure that I believe you, Mr. Lead-up-the-garden-path, but I do know that I don't like you; however, the wellbeing and reputation of this university are my top priorities, so you can be damn sure that I'll look into this matter and take the appropriate action."

Chapter 11

Weston recut the pizzas at the dining room table as Lance, Becky, Ance, and H.P. sat waiting for their slices. "I've grown rather fond of the local pizza offerings, especially these garbage pies, but I wish they'd leave the takeout pizzas uncut like they do in the city. It's a long drive from the pizza parlor, and the cheese inevitably remelts, obscuring the demarcation between slices—not to mention allowing the oil from the pizza to seep into the box and onto any surface upon which it's set."

"But you did mention," said Lance. "You mention it every time we order pizza. You're getting repetitive in your old age."

Weston held up the pizza cutter as he took Lance's plate. "At least I have an excuse for my repetitiveness, whereas you keep repeating the same ageist jokes."

Lance accepted the plated pizza slice from Weston, but not the criticism. "My jokes about you may have the same ageist theme, but they're not the same jokes."

"That's true," agreed Becky. "Just this morning he was making fun of the hair that grows on your ears."

Weston set two slices of pizza on Becky's plate. "I recall not so very long ago you saying that you liked my downy ears. I see now that the feelings of a woman are transitory at best and disingenuous at worst."

"I wasn't the one making fun of your ears." Becky began cutting up one of her pizza slices for Ance.

"Besides, if I was going to tease you about your depilatory regimen—or lack thereof—I'd start with your back hair."

"Ick…Mom," Lance protested, "I'm trying to eat here."

Weston shook his head as he served H.P. a slice of pizza. "See what I have to put up with. First Slim and now my own family…he had the temerity last night to call me Don Wrinkles."

"With your crow's feet," H.P. replied, "I get the wrinkles part but not the funny bit."

"I don't have crow's feet."

"No," said Lance, "more like owl talons."

"Any wrinkles I have are a mark of wisdom like the wizened old owl." Weston patted his daughter on the head. "We forfeit our youth to our children."

"Hap birfday, pa da," Ance cooed.

"Thank you, sweetie, but it's not my birthday." Weston sat down with his own slice of pizza. "It's a thing she's been saying lately." Weston turned from H.P. to Becky. "If she keeps it up, I'm sure mother superior will want to bring in a chronological therapist."

Becky rolled her eyes as she looked over at H.P. "Ance's parochial daycare is under new leadership, and they've started bringing in an occupational therapist once a week to work with the kiddos, which for some unknown reason vexes my husband no end."

Weston began speaking despite his mouth being full of pizza. "It's ridiculous is the reason. She's a toddler; her occupation is to toddle, which she does just fine."

"She mostly helps Ance with her coloring," continued Becky.

"As if that's any sort of occupation." Weston wiped

his mouth. "Like her crayon skills would ever prevent her from getting a job."

"She could grow up to be a colorist," Lance said. "That's a job title I've seen listed in those old comic books H.P. gave me."

"That's right." H.P. nodded. "I hope you're enjoying them."

"He reads them all the time," said Becky. "Sometimes when he's supposed to be doing his homework."

"Schoolwork must come first," H.P. said, "even when you're my age. I always grade my students' stories before reading what I want to read."

"So you'll be back at it in the fall?" asked Becky.

"Yes...though I've been thinking the past few weeks that I may've taken off too much time. I've been struggling to fill the hours of late."

Weston nodded. "He was so hard up for something to do today that he drove all the way over here just to talk to me."

"And while I was here, I received some regrettable news, so Weston asked if I wanted to stay for dinner. I hope it wasn't an imposition."

Becky shook her head. "Not at all. Before we were married, it would've slipped his mind to mention that we were having dinner guests, but he's gotten better about letting me know these things ahead of time, so I guess you can teach an old dog new tricks. It wasn't any trouble to pick up pizza on the way home...and he also told me about your news—sorry to hear it."

"It wasn't all sorrow and sad faces this afternoon," said Weston. "We also workshopped H.P.'s latest writing project."

Becky rolled her eyes again. "Yeah, I saw the evidence of all your hard workshopping when I pulled into the garage—haven't seen the Ping-Pong table cleared off in quite a while."

Weston grinned. "We figured a few spirited matches might help to get the creative juices flowing."

H.P.'s cellphone began vibrating. "My apologies…I should've turned this thing off for dinner." He pulled his phone from his pocket and noticed the caller. "It's my dean actually. Let me quickly take this; he might be calling to ask if I'm available to teach during the summer term." He rose from the table and stepped into the living room. "Hello, I was just thinking of giving you a ring…oh, that's a surprise…I understand, it's not personal…sure, we'll reevaluate at the end of next semester." H.P. returned his phone to his pocket and stepped back into the dining room. "Today seems to be the day for dispiriting phone calls. The dean, at the behest of the chancellor, just informed me that someone else will be teaching my classes in the fall."

Chapter 12

Slim watched as his opponent pocketed the eight ball in the corner. "Nice shot, sarge. Want to shoot another?"

The off-duty officer tipped his brown Stetson hat up to get a better look at the clock on the wall behind the bar. "Nah, I've got to get home before the wife changes the locks on the house...married life—it's like having two jobs."

Slim returned his pool cue to the rack on the wall. "I hear you...but still, it's nice to have somebody to come home to."

"You ever think about getting hitched for a second time, partner?"

"Sure," answered Slim. "All the time I think about how I ain't ever gonna go through that again."

"Marriage is like anything else—benefits and drawbacks. The trick is to focus on the one and forget about the other." The cowboy cop slapped Slim on the back. "Don't stay out too late. We've got work in the morning."

"10-4." Slim returned to the bar to find his usual stool occupied by someone he didn't recognize. He sat two stools down from the young stranger.

"You want another?" asked the bartender.

"Sure, one more for the road."

The bartender set a beer on the bar for Slim and then

turned to the newcomer. "How 'bout you, son—ready for another?"

Mr. Lead shook his head. "I should shove off after I finish this one."

"I ain't see you in here before," Slim said.

"I ain't never been in here before," Mr. Lead replied. "Is it always this dead?"

"Dead…why, you're catching us on one of our busier nights." The bartender turned his attention to the Boutonniere's only other customer seated at the far end of the bar.

"So are you new in town?" asked Slim.

"Yep, doing a little reconnaissance of the area. I just got out of the service and am looking for someplace to set up camp. I hear the cost of living is pretty low down here compared to upstate."

Slim took a swig of beer. "That's true enough, though you gotta factor in that there ain't many jobs around and most of them don't pay so well…but it ain't a bad place to live—lot of good folks in these parts."

"You know the area fairly well then?"

"I've been a cop here for over ten years now…grew up here too. What branch of the service were you in?"

"Coast Guard," answered Mr. Lead, "stationed mostly in the Great Lakes region…just like Grandad."

"Ah, family business…yeah, my daddy was an airman back in 'Nam, and I was an aviator myself, though I never saw any action like him—mostly flew cargo-type prop planes."

"You still do any flying?"

"I got an old Cessna 150."

"A true classic."

"Thanks…leaks a bit of oil though."

"My name's Lead, by the way. My friends in the Guard called me Lead the Reed on account of me being tall and thin like the plant."

"Ain't that a coincidence—my friends call me Slim for the same reason...though I ain't as skinny as I used to be when I was your age."

Mr. Lead swallowed down the last of his beer and set the bottle on the bar as he stood from his stool. "It was good meeting you, Slim...maybe I'll see you around."

Slim nodded. "Yeah, see you around, Reed."

****

Slim exited the bar and walked to his pickup parked in the nearly empty gravel lot. He stepped up into the cab and turned the key in the ignition. The motor roared to life, but when he toggled on the headlights, nothing happened. He got out and walked to the front of his truck—both lights busted. Slim knelt down to inspect the shards of plastic that littered the ground. He never saw the blackjack coming.

Chapter 13

Weston leaned back in his recliner with his laptop on his lap in the hopes that being slightly farther away from the screen would somehow make it seem less empty. He stared at the blank screen for several minutes. *Dammit, H.P., all your talk of writer's block must've rubbed off on me.*

Weston's phone vibrated on the arm of the recliner. He snatched it up—grateful for the distraction. The screen showed it was That Sister calling. "Hey, Kim, Becca's not here right now."

"I know, genius—it's the middle of the day. She's probably either at work or having a nooner with an age-appropriate lover. Don't you think if I was trying to reach her, I would've called her cellphone?"

"It's been great catching up, Kim. If you'd like to chat again sometime, please hesitate to call."

"Have you seen Slim?"

Weston noted the change in his sister-in-law's tone of voice. "I had a couple beers with him at the Boutonniere the other night."

"Not last night?"

"No, H.P. was over last night."

"Maybe you should try spending time with your family for a change instead of always hanging out with your drinking buddies."

Weston did his best to focus on all the times his

sister-in-law had babysat for them on the weekends so that he and Becky could have an evening to themselves. "Was Slim supposed to stop by last night?"

"You mean my place…why would he stop by here?"

"Kim, if you want to keep your little dalliance with Slim a secret, then I'd advise telling him not to leave his truck parked in front of your house overnight."

The line was silent for a moment. "Does Becky know?"

"I don't think so."

"Thanks for not mentioning it to her."

"Don't mention it."

"Correct," Kim said crossly, "don't mention it to her."

"I won't, but I don't understand why you two are sneaking around. I'm sure Becky would prefer that you dated someone who's more into NPR rather than the NRA, but Slim's way better than all the other losers you've dated since I've known you. For starters, he has a job—he actually gets paid to spend time at the police station, unlike your old boyfriends."

"I know…he's a good guy. If my sister knew, I'd be afraid that if things don't work out with him the way these kinds of things usually don't work out for me, then I wouldn't be the only one who was disappointed."

"I hear you, Kim, but it's not like your sister has had the best of luck with men either."

"No kidding—look who she's with now."

"So ta-ta then."

"Wait…so you haven't talked or texted with him today?"

"No, I haven't heard or read from him since we had beers two nights ago. Did you try calling the station?"

"I called the station; I called his cellphone like a dozen times; I even called that old farmer who owns the barn he keeps his trailer parked next to—his truck isn't there. I'm starting to get worried."

"Okay, Kim, even though I'm right in the middle of a feverishly productive writing tear, I'll stop what I'm doing and go look for him."

Chapter 14

Slim awoke with a sharp pain at the base of his skull accompanied by a dull, throbbing pain just about everywhere else. He tried to rub his temples, but his hands—along with the rest of him—were tied to a chair. The changeable letter sign of the donut shop across the street caught his attention: Have you tried our new additions?

Mr. Lead pulled the curtain shut over the large picture window, casting the motel room into darkness. "The sign might as well read: Have you tired of your new addictions? Ought to be as illegal to sell junk food as it is for drug dealers to sell their junk."

"I myself enjoy starting the day with a good donut and a strong cup of coffee." Slim's eyes tried to focus on the voice in the corner of the room.

"Occupational hazard for a cop, I suppose. Do you ever miss it?"

"Miss what…waking up in my own bed with a headache caused by drinking too much rather than getting bushwacked?"

Mr. Lead shook his head from near the door. "No, the military life—in which exceptionalism is valued— rather than your current civilian life, which gives precedence to mediocrity."

"Seems like you got some real big ideas…mind sharing the biggest one of all and telling me what the hell

I'm doing here?"

"Do you know where you are?"

"I'm not quite sure," Slim answered. "Let me go outside real quick for a looksee to get my bearings."

Mr. Lead chambered the pistol he held. "Do you know where you are, soldier?"

"Yeah, I know this motel. We're on the second floor. I get called here all the time...mostly on the weekends for noise complaints—usually teenagers drinking beer."

"Back before the interstates were built, I bet this place was frequented by tourists—families on their way from here to there, stopping in this little town of yours for a hot meal and a good night's sleep. Now this no-tell motel is filled with degenerates and ought to be burned to the ground—preferably on a night with no vacancies."

"Decent people still stay here," Slim replied.

"I know...one of them was a special lady by the name of Allison. This is the last motel room she reported staying in, according to the association she worked for."

"Allison...who was she to you—your sweetheart or something like that?"

Mr. Lead grimaced. "We were friends is all. We met in the service—joint op. Allison saved my life. I don't mean that figuratively neither—she shot a sniper who had me in his crosshairs."

"The way I understand it, you're too late to return the favor. She was fragged by that association of hers."

"The amusing thing is that they don't think I know that. I came here to finish the job she started—professional courtesy, no mission left undone...and her association is backing my play because some relative of mine who I never met happened to know one of your buddies before I was born. I'm going to burn you and all your friends, and then I'm going to burn them."

Slim let out a long sigh. "Listen, ex-grunt to ex-grunt, I know what it is to have some unpleasant thoughts residing inside your head after time spent in the service…but believe me—these friends of mine are decent people too. There are better ways to honor your comrade's memory than by doing them harm."

"Allison disobeyed a direct order from the association by coming back here to reengage her target, and they killed her for it. If this assignment was that important to her, then that's how important finishing it is to me. However, I'm not a soldier without honor. I'll give you and your friends a chance for a final farewell…the kind me and her never had. Until then, if it makes the waiting any easier, take it as a compliment that I chose to go after you first. I figured you for the hardest target in the bunch…though considering the softness of the others in your clique, it's not so much to brag about."

Chapter 15

Weston stepped out onto the front porch when he heard H.P. pull up the driveway. He got into the idling car. "I appreciate you coming with me."

"As you're aware, I have surfeit of free time these days." H.P. backed out of the driveway.

"Couldn't get any writing done this morning?"

"Actually, I typed out a few pages...then realized the scene was almost an exact retelling of the opening from one of my early Pirate Hunter books."

"I say run with it." Weston adjusted his seat. "I doubt many of your readers will remember it...though on the other hand, if they do, you may not want to remind them of your early offerings—stinko."

"I appreciate the vote of confidence."

"All I'm saying is that you've come a long way as a writer—from crap-tastic to capable, and I'm sure one day you'll even progress to consummate...that is, if you live into your late hundreds." The glove compartment door popped open onto Weston's knees. He closed it firmly, but the door soon fell open again, so he stretched out his legs and let it dangle. "I forgot what a piece of junk your car is."

"It's in better shape than yours these days."

"Maybe...maybe not. By now, mine might've been melted down to make a newer model. Perhaps we ought to buy a pair of cars together—you know, get a rate."

"If I don't start getting a steady paycheck again soon, then this heap is all the car that I can afford—with or without a rate."

"Didn't you used to be a millionaire? How'd you spend all your money…clearly not on that dump of a farmhouse. Speaking of, did you stop by Slim's to see if he ever made it home?"

H.P. shook his head. "No sign of his truck—I walked back to the barn and knocked on his trailer door, but no answer."

"I called the station, and the desk sergeant told me he didn't show up for his shift this morning or call in sick, which is out of character."

"So where are we going to start looking for him then?"

"The Boutonniere, I guess."

"It's still early," said H.P. "Maybe we'll be lucky, and they won't be open yet."

****

Finding the bar closed, Weston and H.P. combed the parking lot. H.P. stooped over a patch of gravel. "I feel like we ought to have magnifying glasses for this sort of thing."

Weston felt the back of his neck getting sweaty in the afternoon sun. "For what…burning ants? We're not looking for bread crumbs here."

"Well, what exactly are we looking for then?"

"A clue, of course."

"Care to be more specific?"

"You'll know it when you see it," answered Weston, "though this time I have no idea what size it'll be in relation to a bread box."

Something glinted among the gravel. H.P. picked up

a pellucid piece of plastic. "I think I might've found one of your so-called clues...maybe a fragment from a headlight."

"Are you sure it's not part of a broken bottle?"

"It's clear and sharp...but definitely not glass."

Weston walked toward H.P. to investigate further, but then they both turned as a pickup pulled into the parking lot. The truck parked near the door, and the bartender got out. "You boys must be thirsty. I don't usually get my first customers until about an hour after I open."

"Then why don't you open an hour later?" asked Weston.

"Oh, it's you—the wiseass...and you brought your boyfriend, I see. I remember him from before."

Weston turned to H.P. "Why's he so memorable?"

"Because he tipped me a hundred bucks last time he was here. You tend to remember a tip like that in a place like this."

"We're looking for our friend, Slim," said H.P.

"He ain't here," replied the bartender.

Weston nodded. "Yes, we've determined as much. Was he here last night?"

"Yeah...shot some pool, drank some beer—the usual."

"With anyone unusual?" asked H.P.

"We don't get too many unusual people out here...at least unfamiliar people, I mean. Although now that you mention it, he did chat with this younger guy at the bar just before he left, but don't get excited—I don't think it was any kind of homosexual thing like with yous two."

Weston took a step toward the bartender. "What can you tell us about the young man?"

"Hey, don't you two still owe me a flashlight from last time you both was here?"

Weston took a fifty-dollar bill from his wallet. "I think this ought to cover it."

The bartender accepted the money. "Your boyfriend gave me twice that much before, but then this is still the second-biggest tip I ever got. He wasn't here long…had only the one beer as I recall, but he did say he'd been in the military—don't remember which branch."

"Did he happen to mention his name?" Weston asked.

"Reed, I believe is what he told Slim…or was it Lead—hell, you know I drink on the job, right?"

"I once knew a Mr. Lead," H.P. said, "an old friend and raconteur who taught me a lot about storytelling."

Chapter 16

H.P. and Weston sat on stools inside the Boutonniere, drinking beers as the bartender swept the barroom floor.

"So we know Slim's not at work, not at home, and not at his favorite watering hole," said H.P. "So where does that leave us?"

"Out of ideas," answered Weston. "I wish Ed was here...he'd probably have some off-the-wall theory that'd inadvertently spur a helpful thought."

"When are he and Kate due to return?"

"Not for a few days yet."

H.P. took a sip from his longneck bottle. "Okay...then what about someone else who might also be able to spitball an unconventional hypothesis?"

"Like who?"

"How about that polymath Edwin thought so highly of...Hooper—the one who could calculate the trajectory of an asteroid in his head or whatever."

"Sure, if we knew how to get in touch with him...he's probably shooting pool in some backwater four states away. Besides, I doubt Slim was struck by a meteor."

"Meteorite," corrected H.P. "People are struck by meteorites."

"I'm pretty sure Slim wasn't. What about that vieux barkeep over at the Deluxe? He gave us a good suggestion when we were looking for Ed that time."

"Retired…sold his bar and moved to Florida. I hear the new owners plan to remodel it over the summer— going to reopen in the fall as some kind of swanky gastropub."

"Right, precisely what every college bar needs— sophistication."

"Is there any chance Slim just took off to go hunting or fishing?" asked H.P.

"I thought of that and called his ex-wife, since he usually goes hunting with their son, but he's still in school, and Slim usually calls me if he's going fishing."

"So we haven't got any leads—other than bits of broken plastic that may or may not have been part of the headlights on Slim's pickup—and we don't know anyone who has any better idea than us where he might've gone?"

"That's about the size of it," answered Weston.

"You wouldn't think Slim or his truck would be so hard to find in such a small town."

Weston picked up his beer but then set it back down on the bar. "There's a thought."

H.P. looked around the bar facetiously. "Where?"

"Of all the unlikely places, coming from your mouth. I've been so focused on finding Slim that it never occurred to me that we might be able to find his truck instead."

"Does it have a LoJack?"

"No, but Slim keeps a two-way radio under the passenger's seat that we could use to triangulate its location." Weston shrugged in response to H.P.'s incredulous expression. "I learned about it while doing research for *Station-to-Station Spinster*."

Chapter 17

Mayor McCormick ended the call and set his cellphone on the bar. "Okay, boys, I had the chief of police set up two receiving stations for triangulation, and it seems the signal for Slim's walkie-talkie is coming from this vicinity."

"How big a 'vicinity' are we talking?" asked Weston.

"As the chief explained, his radio should be within a half-mile radius of here—give or take. This isn't like getting a precise GPS location…a lot of variables can affect the signal."

"Maybe he's unconscious in a ditch somewhere nearby," said H.P. "Do you think he might've had a few too many and drove off the road?"

The bartender shook his head as he replaced an empty whiskey bottle behind the bar. "Nah, he didn't drink that much last night. He could've hit a deer or something, but he wasn't drunk when he left here."

"There's only the one road that runs by this place," said the mayor. "We'll start looking a half mile in each direction."

"I drive in every day from the east, and I didn't see no vehicles off the road today," said the bartender.

H.P. nodded. "Yeah, that's the direction we came in too."

"I guess that means we'll start by going the way of

Horace Greeley," said Weston.

****

The mayor drove slowly down the rural road with Weston looking from the passenger's seat and H.P. from the back.

"There," exclaimed Weston. "Those cattails…they look freshly smooshed."

The mayor stopped the car. "Yeah, I guess that's worth checking out."

The three exited the sedan to investigate. They followed the wide trail of bent cattails to a marshy area hidden from the road and soon found Slim's truck resting up to its rocker panels in squelchy mud.

"The headlights are busted," H.P. noted.

"This pickup looks like it's been driven back here and parked," the mayor added, "not like it came skidding off the road."

"But who parked it is the question," said Weston. "I'm fairly certain Slim washes this truck more often than himself. He wouldn't just leave it here."

H.P. opened the driver's side door. "Nothing appears out of the ordinary in the cab."

Weston walked around to the bed of the pickup. "The only thing that's back here is a plastic bag."

"What's in it?" asked the mayor.

Weston slowly opened the flimsy shopping bag. "Paper—handwritten pages…that don't appear to have been written recently."

"Is it a note of some kind…like maybe a ransom note?" the mayor asked.

"No." Weston perused the pages for a moment. "It looks to be a draft of H.P.'s first Pirate Hunter manuscript."

Chapter 18

"You two back already?" asked the bartender, looking up from restocking the beer cooler beneath the bar.

Weston resumed his barstool. "We needed a quiet place to think, and no place quieter came to mind than right here."

The bartender set two beers on the bar. "Did you find Slim?"

"We found his truck," answered H.P. "Off the road not too far from here."

"The mayor dropped us off on his way back to the police station." Weston took a swig of beer. "The chief is sending out a crew to dust for prints and whatnot before it gets dark. They're going to put out an all-points bulletin for Slim."

"You mean an APB?" asked the bartender.

Weston nodded imperiously. "That's correct. I'm sure they'll call if they need us."

H.P. sipped his beer. "I'm positive that the mayor dropped us off here just to get us out of the way."

"If you want to make yourselves useful, you two can keep an eye on the place while I get some more beer from the back." The bartender left the barroom with three empty boxes.

"So what are you thinking?" Weston asked. "Whoever abducted Slim caught him unawares by busting out his headlights then laying in wait for him until he examined the damage, coshing him over the head."

"It's 'lying in wait'…don't you recall my disquisition at your old house just before it burned to the ground?"

"You mean when I was drugged and unconscious—no, I must've missed that one…more's the pity. Maybe we could focus on the matter at hand."

"Quite right," agreed H.P. "Yes, that all tracks with Slim's truck being embosked so close by. The perpetrator could've done the deed, driven Slim and his pickup just down the road far enough to be out of sight, then hoofed it back here on the double to collect his own vehicle. If it was this young man the bartender mentioned, then the entire business could've been accomplished in ten minutes' time."

"That's pretty much what I figured too." Weston spread the few pages of H.P.'s manuscript on the bar for closer inspection. "Your print is lousy, by the way."

"You should see my cursive."

"Why do you think these were in the back of Slim's truck?"

"I have no earthly idea. I received an envelope earlier this week which also contained a page from that manuscript—no letter of explanation or any other information came with it, but clearly someone is trying to tell me something."

"Don't you keep all your old writing in that antediluvian file cabinet of yours in the attic?"

"That's right," answered H.P. "This manuscript was the very first draft in my Pirate Hunter series…the only one that's missing from my collection. I gave it to an old friend of mine in Chicago—the Mr. Lead I mentioned earlier—to read just before I found out it was to be published...never saw it or him again."

"Are you talking about the barfly at that dive you tended bar at when we first met?"

"You may've only known him as a barfly, but he'd lived a full and interesting life. He'd been in the Coast Guard as a young man. In fact, I based some elements of the Pirate Hunter—with his permission, of course—on stories he'd told me of his years in the service, which is why I thought he might enjoy reading it, but I quit that job soon after I got my advance to focus on revisions for that first book. I tried to look him up when the book finally came out to give him a copy, but I learned he'd passed away."

Weston turned over a couple of the pages. "The barkeep told us the young man Slim spoke with was ex-military...it's a stretch, but maybe he's this guy's grandson—idolized Grandpa, wanted to serve in the Coast Guard just like him, then got it into his head somehow that Gramps had written the first Pirate Hunter book based on this early draft that maybe he discovered mixed in with the old-timer's stuff."

"Yeah...pretty stretchy. Instead of kidnapping one of my friends, why not just sue me?"

"Because he's a man of action...or maybe he realizes that the case wouldn't hold up...I'm just brainstorming here. At the very least, I think we can assume that he had a hand in getting your books delisted and your administrative leave extended."

"That seems a safe assumption, though to what end I can't imagine."

Weston held up one of the pages to the light above

the bar. "Why did you underline the word 'Windy'…and here the word 'Cherish'?"

H.P. took the page from Weston to see for himself. "I don't know…I'm not sure that I did."

Weston scrutinized another page. "And on this one you underlined the words 'Love' and 'Never'…and 'My.'"

H.P. studied the two pages side by side as Weston got up from his stool and went to the jukebox. When he returned, the song "Never My Love" began to play. "Do you know who sings this?"

H.P. listened for a moment. "Alice Cooper?"

"The Association."

"That would've been my second guess."

"Do you recall all those times when some goons or other had us tied up?" Weston asked. "They often talked of their 'association.'"

"I always thought I was about to die in those situations…but yes, I do recollect that term being mentioned a time or two. After years of writing about goons, I had no idea what a chatty lot they can be until I had the misfortune to run afoul of them."

"Slim thinks this 'association' isn't just some generic term but rather the actual name of their organization?"

H.P. tilted his head from side to side. "It would make sense to give a clandestine, criminal enterprise a forgettable name. But then why tip their hand with this silly underscoring—not the subtlest of clues. I certainly wouldn't write it into one of my stories…and what does all this have to do with me?"

"As usual, your egocentrism is obscuring your objectivity."

"Well pardon me for being a little self-centered, but you're not the one who just yesterday lost his job and had his life's work invalidated."

"And you're not the one who's missing."

H.P. unfolded his arms. "Okay, that's a good point."

"It seems whoever's behind all this is trying to hit us with a bus while simultaneously throwing this association under that selfsame bus."

"Wouldn't your analogy make him both the bus driver and someone on the sidewalk?"

"We don't have time for your asinine quibbling over semantics now." Weston rubbed his hands together. "If we can find Slim, then I bet we can clear your name in the process too."

Chapter 19

Weston pointed toward the windshield. "See the sign for the donut shop up ahead…the motel parking lot is on the left."

H.P. pulled into the lot and parked near the diminutive office. "This is the fourth motel we've been to in the past hour…are you sure this is a wise use of our time?"

"As opposed to drinking beer while who knows what is happening to Slim?"

"I want to find him as much as you, but our current course of action seems like…" H.P. stopped midsentence as he took the key from the ignition. "I won't say a shot in the dark, because I don't want to hear the theory again about the cave and waiting to see what runs out, but if this is such a smart strategy, then why don't you suggest it to the cops, who're undoubtedly just as invested in finding Slim as us?"

Weston unbuckled his seatbelt. "Because they'd go about it in their inimitable cop way…flashing their badges and demanding answers. A significant percentage of the people who stay in motels like this are probably on the lam; the proprietors of these places know that and aren't too keen on developing a reputation for turning over their clientele to law enforcement, but if we go in there and ask the right questions then we have a better chance of getting the answers we're looking for.

We learned from the investigations after the encounters we've had with association members that staying in cheap motels is part of their modus operandi, so it stands to reason that this guy is following the same playbook."

"It makes sense the way you explain it out here, but somehow it doesn't make sense when we actually go inside and talk to the desk clerk. Why don't I wait in the car this time?"

"Our story only works if we go in together," said Weston. "Makes it seem all the more—"

"Pathetic?" H.P. huffed.

"I was going to say plausible."

The two exited the car and entered the office. The bright Vacancy sign in the window cast a pallor into the small space. The clerk looked up from the tiny television on his desk. "You gents looking for a room. I got a double available, or if you want to pay a bit extra, I can let you two singles."

"We're not looking for a room but rather someone who might be occupying one of them," said H.P.

The clerk looked from H.P. to Weston. "This ain't really the type of place where people come to be found."

Weston shook his head. "The person we're looking for isn't in any kind of trouble…you see, we're his dads."

This time the clerk looked from Weston to H.P. "Okay."

H.P. nodded. "We just found out our son flunked out of med school. We think he might be hiding here because he's too embarrassed to tell us."

"We put a lot of pressure on the boy," added Weston, "wanted him to be a successful surgeon like us."

The clerk looked circumspect. "You both are gay doctors?"

"Well, he's gayer than I am," H.P. answered, "but yes, and now our careers mean nothing to us. We want our son to know that the family business doesn't matter anymore...we just want our boy to come home."

"He's got hair not so very similar in appearance to the man pictured here." Weston opened his wallet and pulled out another fifty-dollar bill. "His name is Lead, but he may be using Reed as an alias."

The clerk eyed the money. "That ain't much of an alias."

"He's real clean cut," H.P. added, "looks like the sort that might be in the military."

The clerk took the fifty-dollar bill. "I don't know nothin' about them names you mentioned...but there's a guy staying here who fits that description—clean cut kinda sticks out in this place. He's in room 211...up on the second floor."

Weston and H.P. left the office and headed for the stairs. Weston turned to H.P. as he climbed the first step. "I think you had a good idea earlier...why don't you wait in the car while I go knock on the door."

H.P. looked up at Weston. "You're afraid we're going to get shot at, aren't you?"

"No, it's not that, but what if this guy makes a run for it? We'll have a better chance of catching him if one of us is waiting in the car to give chase, and since it's your car..."

H.P. pulled his keys from his pocket. "That makes sense, though part of me still thinks you want to go up there alone out of some mistaken sense of nobility."

"You've known me a long time. Over the years have I exhibited a pattern of acting nobly—by mistake or otherwise? I've been shot twice before. If I thought using you as a human shield might prevent me from being shot a third time, I'd invite you up to do the knocking, but what's more likely is this guy's going to rabbit, and I don't want to track him down all over again."

"All right, but I'll never forgive you if you die…especially while doing something heroic."

Weston grinned. "Don't worry, I'm probably going to die the same way as you—slumped over a writing desk."

H.P. returned to his car as Weston continued to climb the stairs. He located room 211, cautiously approached the door, then took a step back so that he stood in front of the room's large picture window with drawn curtains rather than the door itself. Weston extended his arm past the doorframe and knocked thrice.

"Who's there?" a voice from within demanded.

"Room service," answered Weston.

Two shots rang out, leaving bullet holes in the door. Weston hit the deck and heard the window above him shatter. Covered in glass and curtains, he felt two feet land on him and then run off. By the time he pulled himself up to the railing, the assailant had made his way to the bottom of the stairs. Weston watched helplessly as the young man dashed to a late-model coupe and squealed his tires out of the parking lot.

H.P. took off in pursuit, but Weston figured that the old jalopy didn't have much chance of overtaking the newer car—besides, H.P. wasn't quite the same caliber of wheelman as his Pirate Hunter. Weston turned his attention to the room, using the chair that had been thrown through the window to climb inside.

"Slim, you in here?" Weston heard a muffled response from behind the bathroom door. He slowly pushed open the door to find his friend bound with rope in the overfull bathtub. "You okay?" He pulled the strip of duct tape from Slim's mouth.

"I'm a might waterlogged."

"Helluva of a time to take a soak."

Slim nodded to the clock radio set precariously on the edge of the tub. "You mind unplugging that for me?"

Weston pulled the power cord, which stretched across the narrow bathroom, from the socket above the sink, then noticed the string that ran from the radio to the ropes around Slim's torso. "Fairly ingenious—struggle to get free and you run the risk of electrocution."

As Slim sat up, the alarm clock splashed into the water. "Let's not give our bad guy too much credit. He did just run out of here down into what I assume is a parking lot full of police." Slim frowned. "Wait…why were you first in the door?"

"Now hold on, H.P. and I were staying out of trouble at a bar, just like you've always told us to do in these types of situations, but then it occurred to us…mostly H.P., that—"

"How many times do I have to tell you—" Slim interrupted.

"What…'thanks for saving my life'? I figure a few dozen ought to suffice."

Chapter 20

Slim held a steaming coffee mug with both hands as his clothes tumbled inside a dryer in the motel's laundry room. Weston sat across the folding table from him, watching through the front window as police officers questioned the desk clerk and looked for evidence in the parking lot. H.P., pacing in front of the washers and dryers, ended his call and returned his cellphone to his pocket.

"What'd Morty have to say?" asked Weston.

"I finally got him to admit he delisted my books under duress," answered H.P. "He told me Mr. Lead, grandson of the fellow I knew all those years ago, threatened him with litigation if he didn't."

Weston crossed his arms. "So is he going to relist your books now that Mr. Lead—the known kidnapper who we just learned went AWOL from his Coast Guard unit last week—has died a fiery death?"

H.P. nodded. "Yes…and I imagine my dean will call to express a similar reversal once news reaches the chancellor."

Slim sipped his coffee. "That was damn convenient of this Mr. Lead character to leave his wallet with his military ID behind on the nightstand in the room when he ran off…for that matter, it was awful considerate of him to drive himself off that bridge, causing his car to explode on the railroad tracks below the way it did."

"I was chasing after him," said H.P.

"Didn't you say in the statement you just gave to my chief that he was nearly a quarter mile ahead of you by that point?" asked Slim. "He didn't strike me as the type to panic and drive head-on into a guardrail."

"Maybe the fire had already started inside the car when he lost control," said Weston. "From his preliminary investigation, the fire chief thinks accelerants caused the explosion…or at least exacerbated it."

"Perhaps he had combustibles inside his vehicle for whatever he was planning next," H.P. offered. "You told us that he mentioned abducting you was just the first part of his plan, right?"

"Yep," Slim answered, "he did mention that…conveniently."

Weston gestured toward the window. "And the license plate the clerk has on file…your guys told us they already traced it back to a rental agency. You know as well as I do that when they drill down, they're going to discover that it was rented with a credit card belonging to some dummy corporation—similar to the one Allison Belched used, meaning it was more than likely issued by the same association."

"10-4," said Slim. "That all adds up…real convenient like."

"I'm starting to see Slim's point." H.P. leaned against a washing machine. "It's not like this would be the first time someone we thought was dead turned out not to be."

Weston rolled his eyes. "Listen, I'm as skeptical as the next guy—"

"You're more of a cynic than a skeptic," interrupted

H.P.

"Whatever, all I'm saying is that we should take the win here—we've simply gotten better at this sort of thing…this isn't our first rodeo."

Slim stood up, holding onto the towel that almost wrapped all the way around his waist. "Weston, I can't say as I agree with your outlook, but I do appreciate you trying to convince me of it by sounding country like. You two have done enough for tonight—good work…your efforts are much appreciated, but now it's time to go on home."

"What are you going to do, Slim?" asked H.P.

"Policework," answered Slim, "but first I'm going to get my jeans outta this here dryer so I can properly conceal Boss Hogg and the Duke Boys."

Chapter 21

Allister changed the dressings that covered the road rash running up and down his forearms, gingerly rewrapping the wounds in clean bandages. *Better to have road burns from jumping out of the car than the actual burns Mr. Lead's body must've sustained from staying inside it*, thought Allister as he pulled his shirtsleeves back down to his wrists.

Allister leaned back on the couch and looked around his shabby motel room. *What a dump. This place is worse than the last one—though it beats staying in some of the barracks me and Allison have seen in our time.* He hated to think of his sister's final days being spent in such inhospitable environs, but he figured that staying in the same motels she had during her sojourn in and around the small town would help keep him focused—especially now that he'd have to delay delivering the coup de grâce, since he'd learned just after abducting the police officer that one member of Weston's quartet wouldn't even be back in the country for another few days. *That's what Dad always taught us—a soldier's greatest asset is his or her ability to adapt.*

Still, he lamented the ruining of a good plan—all the prep work he'd done to disappear Mr. Lead and keep up his social media presence for the past week so that the Coast Guard and others still believed he was alive, all the research he'd done prior to that to find just the right candidate with a plausible motive for wanting to take out H.P. and his coterie when really it had been Weston who was the true target. Weston had been the one Allison had inveighed against to her association contact—the one who'd made her last assignment personal.

Allister opened the binder that contained copies of the reports Allison and other associates working cases involving Weston and H.P. had filed with the association as well as transcripts from their check-in calls with their handlers. His sister's reports had been what he wanted from the association all along—those and the other thing—and they'd gladly handed them over for a concocted story of revenge and a promise to do their dirty work for them.

Allister shook his head as he flipped through the pages for the umptieth time. Reading her reports made him feel closer to Allison, despite their many years of estrangement. He still couldn't wrap his head around the irony of being so like his older sister, having followed her into the same line of work even, and yet somehow she'd forged a tighter bond with their younger half sister who was so very different from them both—from their father. He'd seen Allison less and less frequently over the years when his mother remarried, as his father continued to move them from base to base. After each visit with his mother and sisters, he'd feel more removed from them—and yet never any closer with his dad.

Allister had always thought that after the military, he'd make an effort to reconnect with Allison—maybe even relocate to the same city as her; however, a few weeks before his hitch was up, he'd received word of his sister's passing. It had taken him months of digging to discover how she'd died, what she'd really done for a living, and for whom. Then the real work began.

Allister imagined the endgame—how gratifying that last moment would be. Nothing could bring Allison back or mend their childhood, but he believed that killing Weston and his cronies together could set things right between them. He closed the binder and rubbed the bridge of his nose. He needed sleep—to clear his mind for a while so that he could devise a new plan or perhaps revise the old one. Suddenly a siren roused him from his woolgathering.

That's not a police siren, or any type of siren for an emergency vehicle. Allister studied the midmorning light coming through the cheap curtains then looked over at the alarm clock on the nightstand whose angry, crimson numbers displayed ten o'clock. *It's Tuesday...the first Tuesday of the month—that must be when this township conducts the monthly test of its emergency warning system.* Allister grinned as an inchoate plan began to take shape in his mind.

Chapter 22

Becky watched her husband as he scrutinized the lunch menu at the Salsa Cauldron. "What are you looking for? You always order the same thing."

Weston looked up. "Do you think they'd make me a chimichanga?"

"Is it on the menu?"

"No, but burritos are, and they deep fry their chips, so all I'd be asking them to do is take a burrito and drop it in the fryer for a minute."

Becky made a moue of disagreement. "Seems a little culturally insensitive to tell them how to prepare their food."

"What if you told them? You're part Hispanic."

"The part of me that's Latina is the part that thinks it'd be culturally insensitive. Why don't you just order your usual burrito? It's not like you need more fried food in your diet."

"Sounded good is all." Weston turned the menu over. "Should we order a pitcher of margaritas?"

"I have to go back to work after this—you know, where I help people with substance abuse issues—so I don't think smelling of tequila would be a great idea."

"Okay…just a thought."

H.P. pointed to Slim as the two approached the table. "Look who followed me into the parking lot…for a moment there I thought I was being pulled over."

Slim sat down across from Weston and Becky. "You might be if you don't get that busted taillight of yours fixed."

H.P. took a seat next to Slim. "I think at this point it makes more fiscal sense to buy a whole new car than to fix all the things that are broken on my old one."

"Entertaining thoughts of buying a new car again," said Weston. "I take it you heard from your dean this morning."

"Indeed, he called to express the chancellor's apologies for the whole misunderstanding—funny how she never expresses those apologies herself—and that my services would once again be required come the fall term."

"Didja get a chance to email her that picture I sent you?" asked Slim.

H.P. nodded. "I emailed the headshot from Mr. Lead's military ID to both her and my publisher. She hasn't gotten back to me yet, but Morty called to say that it more or less looked like the same guy—same haircut, at least."

"Right," said Slim, "the bartender over at the Boutonniere told me the same thing."

"But what about you?" asked Becky. "You had a conversation with him, didn't you?"

"A short one…right before I got clonked on the noggin." Slim reflexively rubbed the back of his head. "I mean the picture doesn't not look like the same fella, but I don't feel comfortable calling that a positive identification."

"Speaking of 'short,' " said Weston, "you looked a little shorter in stature walking in here. I don't believe I've ever seen you wear anything on your feet before but those cowboy boots of yours."

Slim shook his head. "Bastard took my boots and the gun my daddy give me that I kept inside 'em...been wearing my old basketball shoes—feels like I got tire tread strapped to the bottom of my feet."

"So aside from flatfooted, where does that leave us?" asked H.P.

"Scratching our heads," Slim answered. "We got a bad guy who seems to have gone out of his way to ID himself—even got a positive rapid DNA match for Mr. Lead, which my chief has ordered our department to keep hush-hush until the official autopsy results are released. The feds have established a connection between Mr. Lead and this 'association' organization based on emails sent from a dummy account they traced back to him in which he posed as a former comrade of his, presumably one who'd done work as an associate before. Tracking his credit card purchases, they've been able to place Mr. Lead a few days ago in the locale of where they believe the office to be of one of the high-ups in this association, which all jibes with what he told me."

"But you don't like it," said Becky.

"I'd like it just fine if it weren't served to me on a silver platter," replied Slim. "I prefer to work for my meals."

"I'm sure this cantina wouldn't mind if you went back in the kitchen to fry up a chimichanga for a hungry customer." Weston turned to H.P. "What about you...recall anything more about the grandad of this guy that might help us?"

H.P. inhaled. "No, he probably died when this young man was still in diapers, so I suppose I can sort of see how he could figure that I might've taken his grandfather's stories as the plot for my first Pirate Hunter book."

Weston exhaled. "Especially given how creatively barren you are…what with having written the same character for so many years now."

"And remind me—how many books are there in your Spinster series?" asked H.P. "I recall a number of their alliterative titles, but I can't remember the last time I bothered to tally them all up."

"Did this old friend of yours or his grandson have any other family?" asked Becky.

"None that were close," answered Slim. "We ran a check, and the last member of Mr. Lead's immediate family was his father who passed away recently."

"That's too bad." H.P. sighed. "It's been a long time since I've thought of that old guardsman, though he doesn't seem so old to me now since I'm nearly the age he must've been when I saw him last…I really do owe him a lot. I should've dedicated a book to him ages ago and given a copy to his family…let them know how much he meant to me."

Slim smiled at the approaching waitress. "Yep, it's always a good practice to acknowledge people."

Chapter 23

Weston ran a finger along the hood of a sedan in the showroom. "I've never seen this color on a car before. What do you suppose it's called?"

"I'm guessing electric eggplant," replied H.P.

"I don't remember new cars being so shiny...I can see my reflection."

"Reflecting your image will probably cause this vehicle to depreciate in value."

"I'm really glad you clarified depreciate with 'in value'...otherwise I wouldn't have known if you meant depreciate in charisma or charm or what have you—or, in your case, what haven't you. When the salesman comes over to dicker with you about the price of this car, be sure the amount he quotes is in dollars and not donuts."

"I thought we were car shopping for you, not me. The university has threatened to put me out of a job twice in the past six months. I should probably wait until I actually start getting paychecks again in the fall before I take on a car payment. You're the one with insurance money burning a hole in your pocket."

"Trust me, it's not that big a hole." Weston kicked the sedan's tires. "It turned out I had the wrong policy. I thought I was covered for a classic car, but I was only paid for an old one. I doubt the check my insurance company cut would even cover the down payment on this ride."

"Having limited means sort of takes the fun out of car shopping, doesn't it?"

"Yeah, but window shopping still beats working...poor Slim and Becca, a brief break for tacos and then back to the grind."

H.P. continued to peer through the passenger's side window. "That'll be me again in a few months, and frankly I welcome the structure. I don't know how you keep yourself occupied."

"By doing as I please when it pleases me to do so...and what structure are you talking about exactly? Don't you usually teach three classes a semester? Doesn't that add up to like nine actual classroom hours a week—most people work that in a day."

"There's a little more to it than that."

"Do you even go to campus every day?" Weston looked up at the approaching salesperson. "See, this pitiable schlub has a real métier, attempting to sell overpriced scrap metal to recalcitrant customers who have no intention of making a purchase."

"Gentlemen, I can tell you both have exquisite taste...this automobile is literally the conveyance of your dreams."

"He and I happen to have very dissimilar tastes," said H.P. "I'm curious, when you say, 'literally the conveyance of your dreams,' do you mean that this car can transport our reveries?"

Weston grinned. "I'm not going to say I love everything about this 'conveyance,' but there's certainly nothing I hate about it—except the color. Do you happen to have this same model in aubergine or perhaps heliotrope?"

Wesley Payton

"I…I'm not sure," stammered the salesperson.

"Looking for a vehicle empurpled as your prose?" asked H.P.

"This is a very expensive convey—er, car. Do you mind my asking what you two do?"

"I spend most of my time breathing," answered Weston, "which I punctuate with occasional episodes of eating and drinking."

H.P. shook his head. "I think he wants to know if either of us can actually afford this dream machine."

"Not me," Weston replied. "My origins are humble, and I've taken a lifelong vow to stay true to my roots. You see, I came up the hard way…born under a bad sign on the wrong side of the tracks, miles downriver from opportunity—privation and misfortune my only companions."

"I'm in education," added H.P. "And creative writing—neither very lucrative vocations, I'm afraid."

"Oh." The salesman turned toward the showroom's floor-to-ceiling windows and espied an unattended couple out on the lot. "Excuse me for a moment, won't you…but if you need anything, just have them page me at the front office. My name is Jim."

Weston watched the salesman walk briskly toward the door. "I'd bet dollars to donuts his name is anything but Jim."

"That's the second time you've used that phrase; I don't think that particular idiom works in this day and age. It cost me nearly twenty bucks the last time I bought a dozen donuts for a faculty meeting."

Weston observed the salesman circling buzzard-like near the couple. "Do you find it ironic that shameful acts are perpetrated by shameless people?"

"Not all…unless you're talking about you and me, in which case I'd feel compelled to revise my answer."

"That fellow has the look of a man who'd defecate on your lawn and then call the homeowners association to report you for not curbing your dog."

H.P. stood on the balls of his feet for a better view. "I believe you're correct…one clearly capable of mal-feces-ance."

"Oh, that's very nice."

"Thanks…I don't like to go scatological too often, but sometimes the situation simply merits it."

"Hey, I've been meaning to ask you…whatever happened to that Lauren Ipsum gal you met at Ed and Kate's wedding?"

H.P. looked across the roof of the low-slung sedan at Weston. "Speaking of Ed, that was an Edwin-esque transition. Why the sudden interest?"

"Honestly, I couldn't care less, but Becca's been bugging me to ask you since we saw you with Vicky over the weekend. You know how it is with married women—always want to know the business of all their single friends."

"You can tell her it was going well for a while, but then it ended the way most long-distance relationships inevitably do."

"How…by meeting up with your former lover for some ô là là at a hotel two years after it's over?" Weston tapped the car's roof. "You pick up Lauren in this little number, and maybe it'd convince her to move a bit closer."

Chapter 24

Allister opened an association-issued laptop like his sister once had and keyed in the encryption code the coordinator had given him. *I'm messaging you to request additional resources.*

Allister waited…and waited, unsure if the message he'd sent was lingering unread in the coordinator's inbox, or if a response had already been typed but the encryption lag was delaying its transmission.

I'm glad you're still alive. We'd been informed by a law-enforcement source in your vicinity that a man fitting your general description, who was wanted in connection with the abduction of a local police officer, had burned to death in a car crash, though no positive identification could be made.

Allister smiled—pleased that the customary glacial pace of a smalltown police investigation meant that he could continue the charade of posing as Mr. Lead for the time being. *Yes, I used a decoy to cover my tracks—a hitchhiker I happened upon. There's no reason either you or I should appear on the authorities' radar.*

Allister considered turning on the television as he waited for a reply, but he decided to stay focused, opting instead to check his phone for updates to the social media sites frequented by a certain TV journalist.

That was very clever, the coordinator eventually replied. *We appreciate you taking measures to distance yourself and us from this incident, though I am curious why you abducted the police officer at all—why not kill him outright?*

Allister quickly typed a response. *I'd intended to use the cop as bait to lure the other three into a trap, dispatching them all at once with the device you'd given me; however, soon after taking him, I discovered via a blog post made by a reporter who I've linked to H.P. that Edwin Hubert is currently out of the country and won't be returning for a few days yet, which delayed setting the endgame in motion, giving Weston enough time to track me to my motel. He got lucky, but now that they think I'm dead, I'm sure to catch them off guard next time.*

Allister sent the message and then instantly regretted it. Rereading his message in the thread, he felt the tone was all wrong. He knew better than to call an opponent who'd gotten the better of him "lucky." Likewise, admitting that he hadn't been aware that one of his four targets was out of the country made him seem unprepared; he should've mentioned how rarely this group appears on social media, probably having been advised to keep their whereabouts off the internet to prevent the online stalking that he was now attempting, and which association members had undoubtedly attempted in the past.

Be careful not to underestimate this group, the coordinator responded, *your words sound similar to some of the opinions expressed by former associates who are lamentably no longer with us.*

Understood—I never make the same mistake twice. Allister poised his fingers above the keyboard, prepared to type more, but then he hit send instead. He thought adding anything else would be prolix. He'd miscalculated, and he'd learn from it—full stop.

I'm glad, replied the coordinator. *Now tell me more about these additional resources that you'd like to requisition.*

Chapter 25

Weston pushed the shopping cart as Becky loaded groceries into the basket. Becky hefted a case of bottled water from a shelf and slid it onto the cart's lower rack.

"Since when do we drink bottled water?" asked Weston. "Our water filter is working fine."

"It's for the storm cellar. I've been meaning to swap out our supplies down there for tornado season. We should get some new batteries too."

"At a supermarket…maybe after we leave here, we could go to an electronics store and buy some bananas."

"I sense that you're attempting to make a point…of some kind."

Weston gesticulated as if delivering an oration at the Lyceum. "My point is that batteries at grocery stores are overpriced."

"Do they cost more than the time and gas it would take to drive across town to Walmart?"

"It's not just about the money—everyone knows that supermarket batteries are overpriced, so they don't buy them, meaning the batteries sit on the shelf for longer, and thus they're likely twice as old and will only be useable for half as long."

Becky nodded. "Okay, that makes sense, but now that we're down to one vehicle, we don't have as many chances to make shopping trips…raising the opportunity cost of driving to Walmart still higher."

"H.P. and I went car shopping after lunch today."

"Did you find anything?"

"I found out that he and that Lauren lady from Ed and Kate's wedding aren't seeing each other anymore."

"Oh, right…I'd forgotten about her, but then long-distance relationships rarely work out. Why'd he bring her up?"

"You know how it is with single men—always bragging to their married friends about how much action they're getting…Lauren kept me warm in winter, then a spring fling with Vicky, blah-blah-blah."

"Huh, H.P. doesn't seem like the type of guy to kiss and tell."

"Trust me, Becca, when it comes to crowing about coital conquests, there's only one type of guy."

Becky placed a bottle of sparkling water in the cart. "If you say so, but what I was asking about is did you find a car that seemed like a viable candidate as the next Wienermobile…sorry, I meant Weston-mobile?"

"New cars are so expensive these days."

"You don't have to buy another luxury sedan like the last one. This isn't Chicago—people around here are duly impressed if your vehicle is rust free and the color of all the doors match."

"I had my previous car for so long that there's a good chance this next one might be the last automotive purchase I ever make. I don't want to rush it and spend the rest of my life driving around in something I loathe."

"Oh brother," exclaimed Becky under her breath.

"I'm sorry Becca, but that's just the way I feel about it."

"No, there at the end of the aisle—it's my coworker."

"The one you can't stand?"

"Shh."

The woman turned from a display of flavored water. "Becky...don't we see enough of each other at the office? And here you are with your new husband."

"We've been married for going on two years now," replied Becky.

"Oh, you're practically still newlyweds. Me and my guy have been married for almost two decades—high school sweethearts."

Weston smiled at the woman. "So you're Sooners."

"Pardon?"

"I've always thought people who marry their high school sweethearts are like Sooners—you know, early settlers."

"Pardon?!"

Becky shook her head. "He's just joking...warped sense of humor—definitely an acquired taste. Have a good evening."

"Yes." The woman grumpily grabbed a twelve-pack of mixed berry. "I hope you have a nice evening too...or at least one of you."

"You know I have to work with her, right?" Becky chastised as they departed from the aisle. "This isn't like the big city where you can say whatever you please because you'll probably never see the person again."

"You needn't keep reminding me where I live." Weston attempted to change the subject as he steered into the next aisle. "Don't you miss the way Ance used to sit in the cart and stare with wide-eyed wonder at all the different items on the shelves? Now when we bring her shopping she only wants us to chase her around the store."

"They grow up fast…unlike you."

Chapter 26

It had taken him most of the morning and part of the afternoon, but Weston finally completed the first paragraph of his penultimate chapter in the manuscript he'd tentatively entitled *Spinster's Swansong*. All H.P.'s talk of ending his Pirate Hunter series had him thinking along the same lines of going out on top—or at least nearer the top than the bottom, though he'd refrained from revealing his intentions until he completed the first draft so that he could fully assess his feelings about the finale. Having observed his friend's wishy-washy approach to sunsetting his most stalwart character, Weston wanted to be absolutely sure before announcing his plan to bid his Spinster adieu.

Weston's cellphone buzzed on the coffee table. He sat up in his recliner to see who was calling. *Jesus, that guy needs to get a life,* thought Weston as he reached for his phone. "What do you want? I'm busy."

"Making good progress with your writing?" H.P. asked.

"Five pages since this morning."

"That's quite impressive, though at that pace I imagine the story's either mostly comprised of chatty filler or dry exposition in need of fleshing out…or perhaps flushing out."

Weston sighed. "Did you call merely to harangue me, or is there some actual purpose to this conversation?"

"I spent my morning doing some online research—mostly on social media. I think Slim's suspicions might be correct. I've reviewed a number of posts made by Mr. Lead, and those of the past week since he went AWOL seem out of character."

"No shit—that's probably why he went AWOL."

"That's just it," replied H.P. "Mr. Lead had many followers and was a prolific poster—lots of interesting ideas, some of them a bit outré to be sure; however, he never expressed any disgruntlement with the Coast Guard. Then suddenly last week he begins inveighing invective against the Guard."

" 'Inveighing invective'…that sounded better in your head, didn't it?"

"Considerably—nonetheless, the tonal change in his posts is pronounced…except where it isn't."

"Meaning?" asked Weston.

"Meaning that all of his other postings that have nothing to do with the Coast Guard, of which there are many, read as if they were written by someone who's completely gruntled—most of them relating to online videogaming, the sort that a lot of my students play."

"So he had some extra time on his hands to play videogames since going AWOL."

"And to plan a kidnapping as well as whatever else he's supposedly been up to?"

"Okay, that's an interesting point."

"Besides," H.P. added, "a number of the recent posts seemed as if they'd been copied and pasted from bits of previous posts."

"So you're thinking Mr. Lead didn't go AWOL—that instead he was killed by someone else who then assumed his identity…both virtually and in real life."

"Each version would support the validity of the other."

"True," agreed Weston. "Although, I can't help but wonder if the scenario you're suggesting might also somewhat assuage the guilt you may have about not letting the family of this young man know how much his grandfather influenced you."

"That had occurred to me too; however, I can't think of a better way to pay my respects to my old friend than to prove that his grandson isn't the deserter and kidnapper he's been made out to be."

"It sounds as if further discussion is in order…perhaps a fresh perspective might also be of benefit."

"You're thinking of Edwin, aren't you?" asked H.P.

"He and Kate are due to arrive tomorrow. Let's fête them here, and when we grow bored of hearing about Ed's astronomy mumbo-jumbo, we can get his take on what's happened over the past week."

Chapter 27

Under the cover of darkness, Allister scaled the slender tower a half mile from the Payley's residence, which held the nearest emergency warning system siren to their house. He fastened the override apparatus to the housing beneath the siren, splicing together the appropriate wires. Then he carefully climbed down as the guywires that kept the tower vertical shuddered in the wind.

At the base of the tower, Allister pulled a remote control from his rucksack. He had a strong signal; the siren was now under his control. He rummaged through the other items the coordinator had overnighted him. The cellphone jammer was military grade, much more powerful than anything he could've ordered online. The remote kill switch would take time to install on the power lines leading to the Payley house, especially on such a windy night. Then he'd have to find a spot on the property to conceal the microwave transmitter, and of course there was still the original device that the coordinator had given him personally.

All told, the heft of his rucksack was substantial. Allister had intended to drive closer to the Payley's place, but while he was atop the tower, he'd spotted three police cars coming from the direction of their house, so he decided to make his way over on foot through the backwoods and fields. *My sister wouldn't have done any less,* Allister thought as he slung the straps of the pack over his shoulders.

As he hiked into the nearby woods, Allister wondered if along the way he'd literally follow in his older sister's footsteps. *Perhaps she came this way when she reconnoitered the area around the house, or maybe she'd taken up a sniper position at some point on one of the bushy knolls I noticed when I did my own reconnoitering.*

All the association documents he'd pored over for the past few days indicated that the Payley home was the de facto meetinghouse for Weston's group. Allister hoped that was still the case. He thought his sister, wherever she might be, deserved the satisfaction of knowing that Weston and his friends met their demise at what they considered to be a safe haven. *Kill 'em where they eat.*

Chapter 28

Becky stood atop the stepstool to reach the salad bowl on the uppermost shelf of the cabinet. "It'll be nice to have a grownup dinner party for a change."

Weston stood below, admiring the view. "You mean you won't miss ketchup and chicken nugget detritus being flung about the dining room."

Becky looked behind her, not having realized where Weston was in the kitchen. "Are you ogling me?"

"Of course not, we're married…I'm simply observing—you know, in case you happen to fall."

"So you can catch me?"

"No, so I can call 9-1-1 and then keep you company while we wait together for the ambulance."

She handed him the salad bowl and stepped down from the stool. "Here—make yourself useful."

The doorbell rang. "I will by letting our guests in." Weston crossed the living room to answer the front door.

"Look who I found at the train station." H.P. moved out of the way so that Edwin and Kate could enter first.

"Aren't you two looking tan?" Weston asked rhetorically.

Edwin offered an awkward fist bump. "Or in my case, sunburnt, which helps to camouflage all my mosquito bites."

Weston nodded. "It seems marriage has done nothing to ameliorate your disdain for the feel of ointments and balms on your skin."

"It has not." Kate hugged Weston. "However, thanks to his wife's good-natured nagging, thus far marriage has resulted in him having slightly less skin."

Weston studied Edwin for a moment. "Yes, it does appear as if you've dropped a few pounds since I saw you last." He noticed Slim standing behind H.P. on the front porch. "At this rate, we'll soon have two Slims in our little group."

Slim entered with H.P. "I hitched a ride on account of those idgets who towed my truck busted the rear axle while pulling it out of the muck."

Edwin sniffed at the air. "I don't think there's much chance of me becoming as thin as this young man if whatever the source of that aroma is tastes as good as it smells."

"Becca made your favorite—vegetarian lasagna."

Edwin rubbed his belly. "Splendid…I haven't had any pasta since we left for our equatorial holiday. It's been a month of Mexican food."

"I don't believe the equator crosses Mexico," said H.P.

"According to my husband—who can memorize star charts but struggles with terrestrial geography—all the cuisine in South America is Mexican."

Weston grinned. "The gastronomic fare notwithstanding, I trust your honeymoon was pleasurable and that all your nocturnal activities involved stiff telescopes that pointed ever heavenward."

Edwin shook his head. "Of course, what use would anyone have for a floppy telescope that points down?"

Kate patted her husband's back. "Eddie, I believe Weston is suggesting that we may've done something a bit more suggestive than stargazing with our evenings."

"Ah, he's quite good at that…yes, for people our age, we engaged in an inordinate amount of sexual congress."

****

Edwin helped himself to a second serving of lasagna while most everyone else at the table had only eaten half of their first. "Becky, this lasagna is delectable—the marinara quite piquant."

"Thank you," Becky replied. "I don't recall my lasagna ever being described as such."

Weston wiped the corner of his mouth with a napkin. "Ed, did the stars look any different from the middle of our planet than they do from the middle of our country?"

"Not so very much, but the long nights gave us ample opportunity for observation."

"However, the most captivating celestial event we saw occurred during the day," Kate added.

"That's right, we witnessed a total solar eclipse that we wouldn't have been able to see from here."

Kate nodded. "Which is the reason we left for our honeymoon several weeks earlier than we'd originally planned."

"Miss Kate, I take it that things are going well at your new job if you were able to leave work for a whole month," said Slim.

"Yes, surprisingly so. Say what you will about Anne Hedonia, but she did a lot to improve the company's day-to-day operations—stepping into her role has been a relatively smooth transition…aside from the fallout caused by the ongoing investigation into her sub-rosa council, though we're weathering the storm."

Edwin swallowed a mouthful of lasagna. "Oh, speaking of women with punny names, Weston I had another thought for a possible female character in your next book—Claire Voyant...perhaps she's a villainess who can read minds."

Weston sighed. "I get it, but frankly that sort of over-the-top wordplay has a very limited appeal for most readers."

"Maybe we ought to ask Ed and Kate their opinion about this Mr. Lead," Becky suggested.

Edwin gulped some wine to wash down his lasagna. "My opinion is that it's a shame Mr. Lead isn't a woman...we could call him Miss Lead, which given the circumstances would seem apposite."

"I caught them up to speed on the car ride over," added H.P.

Kate inhaled deeply. "The prevailing opinion seems to be that this Mr. Lead is not the same person whose remains were found in the recently exploded vehicle, which of course begs the question who is he?"

Edwin set down his wineglass. "Though I think the most pressing questions at the moment are: where is he, and what's he planning next?"

"Agreed," Kate replied. "However, I believe attempting to answer the question I posed may also help answer yours. Slim mentioned the assailant recoiled when he asked if there had been a romantic connection between him and Allison Belched. I find it curious that someone capable of kidnapping one of our friends and derailing the career of another would cringe at a perfectly reasonable assumption."

Becky snapped her fingers. "Unless the suggestion of such a relationship was insulting...like if they had a familial relationship."

"Brother and sister, perhaps," Edwin offered.

Slim took a swig of beer. "So if Allison was this fella's sister, then maybe he's following her same playbook, meaning that this ain't so much about completing her mission as it is about getting her the revenge she was after when she lost her head."

H.P. shook his head. "And just like her, I suspect in such matters he's of the mindset that if at first you don't succeed, try, try again."

"So if I'm hearing you all correctly, he's really after me, and this isn't over," said Weston. "Once again I've managed to put those around me in harm's way."

Becky placed her hand on her husband's. "We're all in this together."

Just then the lights in the house went out.

"We're certainly all in the dark together." Weston pulled his cellphone from his pocket to use as a flashlight.

"Not the first time for that," replied H.P.

"Is anyone else's phone working?" asked Weston. "Mine has power but no signal."

Kate checked her cellphone. "Same with mine."

"Me too," said Becky.

The sudden blaring of an emergency warning siren distracted the rest of the dinner party from checking their mobile phones.

"They must've issued a tornado watch," said Slim. "Becky, you got a battery-powered radio in the house?"

"Yeah…there's one in the laundry room—be right back."

"It wasn't even raining on the way over," said H.P.

Slim made his way to the window. "That's how they

can be sometimes—pop up out of nowhere. Threequarters of all tornadoes in Illinois happen in the early evening hours during springtime. I've heard 'em before as loud as a freight train in the middle of a windstorm or as quiet as a soft breeze on a calm day."

"Do you see anything out there?" asked Weston.

"Just darkness," answered Slim. "The damn thing could be a half mile down the road, and we might not even know it."

"Would a tornado affect our phones like this?" asked H.P.

"Sure," Edwin answered, "if it knocked out a cell tower."

"Should we move to the basement or the center of the house at least?" asked Kate.

Becky returned with the radio. "Our basement is more of a crawlspace that gets wet during a downpour, but we have a storm shelter out back that always stays dry." Becky turned on the radio.

"Repeat: this is an urgent announcement from the National Weather Service. Multiple tornadoes have been spotted for this listening area—seek shelter now."

Becky turned the radio off. "Leave everything, there are supplies in the shelter—follow me."

The six raced for the embankment shelter in the backyard. Slim and Weston held open the angled doors for the others as they descended the cinderblock steps. Then Slim and Weston pulled the steel doors shut behind them with a loud clang. Save for the faint glow of twilight seeping through the small gap between the doors and the sound of people trying to catch their breath, all was dark and quiet. Becky switched on a flashlight and then the radio.

"Repeat: this is an urgent announcement from the National Weather Service. Multiple tornadoes have been spotted for this listening area—seek shelter now."

"Done and done," said Weston.

"So aside from tautologizing, what should we do?" asked Edwin.

Becky dialed down the volume on the radio. "I think there's a deck of cards in here somewhere, though I don't feel much like playing games at the moment."

Slim stood on the lowest step to look through the space between the doors.

"Any change in the weather?" asked H.P.

"None whatsoever." Slim turned toward the others. "Wish I had the two-way radio I keep in my truck so that I could call the station to see what they know."

Something heavy landed on the cellar doors with a reverberating thud.

"Was that a tree branch?" asked Kate.

Slim returned his attention to the gap between the doors, but something partially obstructed his view. He banged on the door with his fist. "Shit."

"Indeed, you're in a world of it now, soldier," a voice called down.

"Who is that?" asked Becky.

"The perp formerly known as Mr. Lead," answered Slim.

"That's correct," said Allister. "I bet you wish you had that snub-nosed revolver you kept stuffed in your bootleg right about now."

"I sure do," Slim replied. "Why don't you drop your piece down between the doors for a moment? I promise I'll return it to you."

"I don't think so."

"So what's your play then?" asked Slim. "I see that you slid something through the door handles to lock us in, but that means you're stuck out there while we're safe down here."

"Safety is such a relative concept," Allister replied. "You are indeed safe from any tornadoes that might happen to pass this way, though in this particular instance that threat is more of a subterfuge than a centrifuge. However, I did place something provocative down there with you, which these steel doors should keep me safe from. You have five minutes until it detonates. See, I'm a man of my word; I told you I'd give you and your friends a chance for a final farewell together before I burned you…but a bit of advice—if you do happen to find what I left behind, I wouldn't disturb it, or you won't get your full five minutes after all. Weston, just so you know, this is both hello and goodbye from Allison."

"When I see her next, I'll be sure to tell her what an asshole her brother is," Weston shouted.

Allister chuckled as he stepped off the door. "I doubt she'll be surprised."

Slim pressed his face against the doors to get a better look through the gap. "He's leaving—probably noticed all the black and whites driving by on a regular basis, so he wants to make himself scarce before whatever's down here with us goes off."

"This water isn't where I put it when I brought it down the other day." Becky lifted a case of bottled water from a stack of canned goods. "I think I found what he left for us…looks like a six-inch cube of modeling clay."

"Is it orange or gray?" asked H.P.

"Orange," Becky answered.

Wesley Payton

"Then it's Semtex," H.P. replied, "not C4."

"Is that pertinent information?" asked Weston.

H.P. sighed. "Not really...one's as deadly as the other. The Pirate Hunter has dealt with them both on various occasions."

"So how would the Pirate Hunter disarm it?" asked Kate.

"Are there any sort of wires or little nodules affixed to the cube?" H.P. asked.

Becky shook her head. "No...it's flat and uniform on all sides."

"That's what I figured," said H.P. "The detonation device is internal...most likely attached to each of the walls, so if we try pulling it apart, it'll trigger the device."

Weston stood up. "Okay, there's no way to diffuse the bomb, so then we need to get out of here before it goes off. Becca, are there any bolt cutters down here or a hacksaw maybe?"

Slim continued to peer between the doors. "That won't work either. Son of a bitch shoved a big ol' Crescent wrench through the door handles and put a padlock in the hole at the end so that we can't slide it out. This thing's made of case-hardened steel; it'd take a blowtorch and time to cut through it."

"Then I'm all out of ideas." Weston rubbed his forehead. "Anyone else got something?"

"Would you mind turning up the radio a little?" asked Edwin.

Becky twisted the volume knob slightly so that they could better hear the pop song playing.

"It's a bit upbeat for a dirge," Weston said. "Are you having a thought, Ed?"

"I believe I am," Edwin replied. "The radio is no

104

longer repeating the tornado warning."

Kate placed a hand on her husband's shoulder. "Eddie, that's because there never was a tornado."

"Right, that miscreant up there most likely overpowered all the radio signals in the area with a microwave transmitter, which broadcast that repeated seek-shelter warning. Apparently, he's since turned the transmitter off, probably because he intends to detonate the bomb via a radio signal."

"That's interesting," Weston replied, "but is it useful?"

"Possibly," answered Edwin. "I used to communicate with radiosondes tethered to weather balloons for research I did back in college using a microwave transmitter. I stowed a box of my non-essential electronics down here when I moved all my gear out of that storage unit in town."

Becky crouched into the corner of the shelter. "I know right where it is. I'd considered throwing it out more than once."

"I'm glad you didn't," replied Edwin. "However, I'm sure the batteries no longer work. Do you happen to have any D-cells?"

"That's what the flashlights I keep in here use," Becky answered.

Weston reached for a package of D-cells on a shelf. "Let's hope these grocery-store batteries still have some juice."

As Edwin rummaged through the box, Weston unwrapped the batteries. Edwin found his microwave transmitter and replaced the D-cells. Then he powered on the device. The transmitter's LEDs lit up. Edwin made several adjustments with dials and toggle switches.

"I set it to full power, which should be enough to block all radio signals in the immediate vicinity…listen."

"I don't hear anything now except static," said Slim.

Edwin grinned. "Exactly, Becky's radio is no longer receiving a signal…though we won't know for certain it'll work to block the bomb's detonation signal until the five minutes have elapsed."

H.P. frowned. "We still have a problem. Detonation devices for plastic explosives that use radio signals are typically line of sight."

"So what's the problem?" asked Becky.

"The problem is that our perp most likely scampered off so he could make his getaway when we go boom," answered Slim, "but he's probably still close enough to see if there ain't no fireworks when he presses the button, in which case he'd almost certainly come back and shoot us dead."

"How big a blast are we talking?" Kate asked.

H.P. inspected the orange block. "There's no telling how thick the faces of that cube are, but even if they're on the thin side, that's still a lot of Semtex…big explosion." H.P. moved toward the doors next to Slim. "But these steel doors are pretty thick themselves…and we are underground."

"What are you thinking?" asked Weston.

H.P. turned to Becky. "Do you keep any flares down here?"

"I think there might be a couple in the emergency kit I've got." Becky quickly pulled two road flares from a vinyl bag and handed them to H.P.

"Perfect," replied H.P., "or at least let's hope it's good enough to look from afar like a conflagration is blazing just behind these doors." H.P. gave one flare to

Slim and began to light the other.

Weston held up his hands. "Wait…was anyone keeping track of the time? Has it been five minutes yet? Won't he get suspicious if the bomb goes off too soon?"

Each of the six turned to the others in cellar, marking the uncertain expressions they saw. Kate broke the silence first. "Light them up."

"But how do you know it's been five minutes?" Weston asked.

"I don't," answered Kate, "but if we're early then he'll just assume we tampered with the bomb."

Weston nodded. "Oh, right…in all the excitement, I'd forgotten about that part."

****

Allister sat in his car across the field, waiting as the second hand on his wristwatch ticked toward the twelve o'clock position when abruptly he became distracted by a bright glow in the distance. He raised his binoculars to his eyes and smirked. Like his sister, explosions always caused him to have an acute visceral reaction. He thought the sparks and flames shooting from between the doors of the storm cellar must be what the entrance to Hell looked like. *Now, Weston, you and your friends are right where I want you.* He started the engine but left the headlights off as he spotted a police car driving toward the house.

Chapter 29

The welder removed the bifurcated Crescent wrench, and the six emerged from the cellar coughing and gasping for breath.

"Jesus, it's good to be out of there," said Weston. "Between the sulfur fumes from the flares and the flames from the blowtorch, it feels like we spent the night in Hades."

The welder removed his protective hood. "Sorry, I would've had you out sooner, but it's not the easiest thing to cut through metal that's resting on metal. If I'd rushed too much I might've welded the doors shut."

H.P. patted him on the back. "We all appreciate you making a house call after business hours."

Slim made his way over to the police chief. "Any trace of the fella who did this?"

The chief shook his head. "The only tire tracks we found up to the house belong to the car in the driveway."

"So he came in on foot," said Slim, "which means he must've parked nearby."

"I've had officers sweeping the area since the first patrolman arrived on the scene when he noticed the flares and radioed in that you all were trapped…no reports of suspicious vehicles."

"Which means the perp probably hightailed it when he saw the patrol car pull up to the house."

"You say that like it's a good thing."

Slim nodded. "I think it might be…likely he drove off satisfied that we burned to death down in that cellar."

"Possibly…I ordered the officers to keep quiet over their radios about what was going on out here."

"I'm sure glad you did. If the perp was listening to a police scanner, he might've figured no news is good news, and a bad guy taking you for dead can be advantageous."

The chief crossed his arms. "Then I guess you better go let your people know that they'll need to lie low for a while, so you can take full advantage of your newfound advantageousness."

"Thanks chief." Slim entered the house. He found the others in the kitchen with empty mugs in their hands, waiting around a brewing pot of coffee.

Becky offered him a cup. "It should be finished in a minute."

Slim accepted the mug. "Under normal circumstances, I'd say it's too late for coffee, but I think our late night is about to turn into an early morning."

"What do you mean, young man?" asked Edwin.

Weston hopped up onto the counter for a seat. "He means that Allison's brother most likely thinks we died, and our best chance of catching this guy is to use that to our benefit, so we have to keep up the illusion of being dead."

"Meaning we can't stay here," added Becky, "and you guys can't go home."

Slim sighed. "Yep, I'm afraid that's what it means all right."

The coffee maker beeped.

Kate inhaled deeply. "Then, Becky, do you have any Styrofoam cups so that we can take this coffee to go?"

Chapter 30

Weston and H.P. surveyed the fishing trophies on the rough-hewn mantel above the fireplace in the rustic farmhouse's living room.

"Which of these do you suppose is the angling equivalent of a Pulitzer?" asked Weston.

H.P. shrugged. "I don't know, but if we were as good of writers as this guy is a fisherman, we'd each have won a Nobel by now."

"What are you talking about? I'm a winning writer...or at least a winsome writer."

Slim approached the pair with a basset hound following closely behind. "The old timer who lives here sold off all his cropland several years ago. Now he spends most of his retirement on his fishing boat. He's down at a tournament in Kentucky—won't be back for a week."

"And he doesn't mind us staying here while he's gone?" asked H.P.

"I called him to make sure—explained the situation. He told me he wouldn't mind remaining in Kentucky an extra week or three to tour some of the local bourbon distilleries if it'd help us out any."

"That's very generous of him." Weston looked about the living room. "I suppose staying here beats bunking at the police station."

"Yeah, and despite having my trailer parked out

back by the barn for going on two years now, I get all my mail delivered to a P.O. box, so there ain't no record of me living out here for our bad guy to look up and drive by to double-check that I'm not still above ground." Slim reached down to pet the dog. "Besides, I agreed to look after old Gus here while his owner's away."

Weston sighed. "So what'll we do while we wait for the authorities to track down whoever's out to get us this time?"

"Well, there's about a thousand hours of fishing videos you can watch, if you're so inclined," offered Slim, "but hopefully we won't have to wait that long. I just got off the phone with the chief, and he had some news to share. Allison Belched did indeed have a brother…named Allister, but I don't think knowing his name is going to do us much good. He's been off the grid since he was discharged from the Army some months back, and he's former special forces—you know, a Green Beret type—with a highly classified record, which means he's likely had extensive training making himself invisible."

"At least we'll know what to call him if we ever cross paths again," Weston replied.

H.P. shook his head. "That never did us any good when dealing with his sister."

"That ain't all the intel I got," Slim continued. "The explosive ordnance disposal team was able to disable and disassemble the bomb Allister left for us. They found a couple of prints inside—thumb and index finger—neither belonging to him."

"Then whose are they?" Weston asked.

"The chief ran them through every database we have access to but didn't get a single hit, which is mighty peculiar in this day and age."

"So what do you think it means?" H.P. asked.

"I think Allister is trying to tell the investigators something," answered Slim. "As I mentioned before, he told me that after doing away with us, his plan was to bring down the association his sister worked for. Given that the fingerprints were found on a Semtex wrapper neatly encased in a little steel container inside the bomb, I'd bet they belong to whoever at the association gave him the explosives."

Weston whistled. "I suppose blowing up six people—two of them writers, one of them famous—would be enough to get the authorities interested in whosever prints those are."

"I guess so," replied Slim, "though the trick now is to figure out whose fingers made those prints."

H.P. rubbed his forehead. "Should we wake the others up and share this new news with them?"

Slim yawned. "Nah, let them sleep a little longer…it was a long night for all of us."

"Besides, it'll be lunchtime soon," added Weston. "Ed's grumbling stomach ought to make for a fairly effective alarm clock."

Chapter 31

When Allister entered the unassuming office, the association coordinator stood and came around his desk to shake hands. "It's good to see you again, son. We got word yesterday that you succeeded in your task, and let me tell you last night I got the best sleep I've had in years."

Allister took a seat. "I'm glad that you're pleased, sir."

The coordinator opened a desk drawer and pulled out a bottle of rye. He set two glasses on the desk and filled each of them halfway full. He handed one across the desk and settled back in his chair with the other. "I propose a toast: here's to a mission accomplished…after all my efforts—all the associates I lost—you, young man, finally managed to kill Weston and H.P."

Allister sipped his rye. "Thank you, sir."

"No, thank you. So what's next? You've certainly proven yourself a most capable operator. I'm sure we could find a role for you in our association."

"I appreciate that, but I feel as if my mission is only half done, and I'd like to one day experience the same restful sleep as you."

"What troubles you, son?"

Allister sighed. "I've been listening to the news reports of H.P.'s demise. I thought killing him and his friends would settle the score, but it seems all I've succeeded in doing is making him into a martyr. His books have become more popular than ever; his publisher even announced that they intend to release new editions of the entire Pirate Hunter series."

"Yes, I'd heard that as well…it's not unusual for artists to become more famous in death than they ever were in life."

"H.P.'s not an artist. He's a hack and a thief. I destroyed the man, but before I can have closure, I need to destroy the man's reputation."

The coordinator sat up in his chair and placed his glass on the desk. "Son, you've done right by your grandad. Based on what you've told me about him, I'm sure he'd be proud of you. In my experience, closure is an illusion. This thing is over—let it be. You're a young man…you should get on with living your own life."

"I feel like I can't truly start my life until all this has been brought to a decisive end, and it won't be finished for me until the world knows what a fraud H.P. was."

The coordinator shook his head. "I'm sorry to hear you say that, son. However, as far as the association is concerned, this matter is concluded."

"I understand, sir."

"Let me know if you change your mind about coming to work for us."

"I will." Allister drank down the last of his rye and stood up to leave but then stopped before reaching the door. "I wonder…could I impose on you one last time for a few resources for the final phase of my plan?"

The coordinator leaned back in his chair again and studied the young man for a moment. "Sure, I suppose we owe you that much."

Chapter 32

Becky held the telephone tightly against her ear as if it might be taken away at any moment. "I love you both so much. Listen to your Auntie Kim. We'll see you soon—I promise." Becky hung up the old-fashioned wall phone in its cradle.

Weston, appearing concerned that she might collapse, pulled her in close. "I know…I know, but it's not like we haven't been away from them before."

"Overnight…not for two days and counting—and not without telling them goodbye first."

"I know, Becca." He let her cry into his shoulder.

Edwin walked into the kitchen with the intention of making a peanut butter and jelly sandwich, but witnessing the emotional scene, he quickly returned to the living room and resumed his seat on the couch.

Kate raised her head from the half-completed jigsaw puzzle on the coffee table. "I thought you were going to make a PB&J."

"There are intense feelings being felt in the other room at the moment."

H.P. lowered his newspaper. "A kitchen is no place for such displays."

Slim looked up from petting Gus on the floor. "This old farmhouse has gotten a might smaller over the past couple days."

"Yes," Kate agreed, "this isn't exactly the return

from our honeymoon I'd envisioned."

Weston and Becky entered from the kitchen. "I think our strategy of waiting for Allister to make the next move has grown untenable. We ought to be proactive instead of reactive."

Becky wiped her eyes. "I need to hug my kids again."

"I've been thinking if Allister duped the association by convincing them that he's someone else, and we convinced him that we're dead, then couldn't we go after the association directly and get to Allister through them?"

Slim stood up. "Weston, I get what you're saying and why you're saying it, but you got to catch the little fish first so that you can use him for bait to then catch the big fish."

Weston rolled his eyes. "We don't need folksy metaphors now, what we need is action. Didn't you tell us that your department kept the identity of the corpse in the car and the fact that we're still alive under wraps?"

Slim nodded. "Yes, on both accounts, and I'd trust my fellow officers with my life, but—"

"No 'buts,' " interrupted Weston. "Allister fooled the association, and we fooled him, so let's go full circle and fool the association into leading us to Allister."

"What you're proposing sounds more like a circle of fools than a full circle," replied H.P.

Weston motioned to Edwin. "The logic is sound…it'll work by dint of—what's it called, Ed, when you move numbers around but still achieve the same result—the Associative Property? That makes sense, right, since we're going after the association?"

Edwin shook his head. "I believe you mean the

Commutative Property."

"Ain't that just another type of metaphor?" asked Slim.

Weston sighed. "True…but it's fancy, not folksy—it involves math, after all."

"What do you have in mind?" asked Kate.

Chapter 33

Allister sat hunched over his computer, wearing headphones and scrutinizing the monitor. In a single day, he'd compiled several hours of video of the association coordinator's comings and goings—mostly footage of him driving; however, his various destinations would certainly be of interest to different levels of law enforcement.

Allister had captured images of the coordinator entering the rear door of a casino alleged to have ties to organized crime. He'd also managed to record a meeting in a deserted parking lot during which the coordinator accepted an envelope from a woman who'd recently been in the news as a suspect in a corporate tax evasion scandal. Finally, he'd videoed the coordinator driving onto the grounds of the Russian consulate.

A pretty high-profile clientele for someone whose office is in a strip mall. He'd edited the video package down to a few minutes, making sure the timestamps in the corner of the screen were in chronological order. He figured the video was short enough to keep the average conspiracy theorist's attention but contained enough detail to help the authorities build an airtight case against the association.

This is going to have the look and feel of a political ad, Allister thought as he began the process of overlaying audio excerpts he'd selected from his meeting with the coordinator from the day before. He'd taken a big risk by surreptitiously bringing in a recording device, but he'd gambled correctly that despite the burly personal assistant having frisked him for his first meeting, the coordinator would give instructions not to bother for the second since he'd successfully completed the mission— all threats seemingly neutralized.

Despite Allister's initial setback of learning that Edwin was out of the country after he'd already set his plan into motion, everything was now running like clockwork. *The timing will still be tight though.* He anticipated that any day the authorities would announce the identity of the burned corpse in the car he'd sent careening off the bridge, and then Mr. Lead's social media accounts would in turn be shut down, preventing him access to the platform he needed to release the video package he was putting together.

However, if Allister was able to post the video before Mr. Lead's social media accounts were locked down, he harbored no concerns about his plan involving the posting of the video after Mr. Lead's demise would eventually be revealed to have occurred. Ironically, the anachronistic release would only further engage the conspiracy-fixated following Mr. Lead had cultivated. *Who knows,* he mused, *perhaps eventually Mr. Lead's online followers will pressure the authorities to examine his presumed ties to the association more than any of my actions will.*

Regardless, Allister had no ties keeping him in the country, so once his mission was completed, he intended to live out the rest of his life as a mercenary overseas and, with a bit of luck, retire while he still retained some of his youth as a gentleman of leisure. *One step at a time, can't get ahead of myself.* After he finished the video and got some kip, he planned to drive back to Weston's hometown for his final task—something that would further rile the small town likely still teeming with agents from several branches of law enforcement investigating the incendiary death of Weston and his friends. Upon completion of what he had in mind, he didn't figure it would take any great apophenic leap to connect those events with the incriminating video he intended to release soon after on Mr. Lead's social media platform featuring the association coordinator.

Chapter 34

Mayor McCormick drove his shiny sedan down the gravel road. He glanced in his rearview mirror, irritated with the dust trail his car made. *I just had her detailed.* He looked up ahead at the approaching storm clouds. He figured his town was in store for a gully washer by the afternoon. *At least dust is better than mud.*

The mayor pulled into the long driveway of a lone farmhouse. He couldn't think of a better hideout for six people who were purported to be dead; the nearest house was almost a mile away. He parked and got out of his car with three pizza boxes in hand. He set the pizzas on the sedan's roof and took a banker's box from the backseat. Something glinting in the sky caught his attention. He scanned the overcast area above him, but he didn't see anything other than gray clouds.

The mayor toted the carboard box and the three pizzas up the front steps. Weston opened the door and stepped out onto the veranda to welcome him. "I saw you drive up. That evidence box sure looks heavy. If we weren't under strict orders to stay out of sight of the road, I'd have come down to help you with it."

"You could take it now," suggested the mayor.

Weston took the pizzas instead. "You've already climbed the steps. The hard part's over...you may as well carry it the rest of the way—on the coffee table will be fine."

The mayor lugged the heavy box into the living room. "I brought lunch everyone."

The other five entered from various rooms. Edwin eyed the pizzas that Weston held. "I hope one of those is vegetarian. I don't eat meat."

"Yes, I believe you may've mentioned that once or twice before," the mayor replied sarcastically.

H.P. pointed to the box on the coffee table. "Is that thing full of documents...I was expecting maybe a folder."

The mayor rubbed his back. "Nope, as you all requested, there's a printout in there of every form and report the police chief and the county sheriff could find pertaining to the events that occurred in these parts involving you all."

Kate whistled. "I know the past couple of years have been fraught with incidents and intrigue, but I didn't think they merited a hernia."

"We've got nothing but time on our hands," said Becky. "We'll comb through everything and see what we can come up with—thanks for bringing it."

The mayor nodded. "You bet...though neither the chief nor the sheriff seemed too optimistic that you'd find anything helpful. After all, their people were the ones who compiled this information, and so far the feds haven't been able to use it to track down Allison Belched's former employer."

"Welp, since we're looking for her brother and not her boss, maybe we'll get lucky." Slim petted Gus on the head. "Even the sun shines on a dog's ass some days."

"Wouldn't the sun shine on a canine's posterior every day that wasn't cloudy?" asked Edwin.

Weston turned toward the mayor. "It's been a trying

few days."

"You're telling me," Mayor McCormick replied. "Because of you six, I've got investigators in town from just about every alphabet law enforcement agency there is, and I'm fielding phone calls from press around the country who're trying to figure out if there really was an explosion involving two mildly renowned writers, and if so who died, and if nobody died how come they keep hearing rumors about government agents in my town…then to top it off, we've got the May Day festival this weekend, and somehow the town's twelve foot maypole has gone missing."

Chapter 35

"Oh, I'm sorry to hear that," said Kate. "Yes, a good day to you too." Kate ended the call on her cellphone and placed the sheet of paper she'd been holding in the now mostly empty banker's box on the coffee table. "Allister and Allison's mother is deceased. It seems she passed away soon after her eldest daughter."

Becky took a sheet of paper from the tall stack next to the banker's box. "I've got a number here for the younger daughter in Seattle...looks like she had a different father."

"Still worth a shot," said H.P. from the recliner as he reviewed documents of his own.

Becky made the call. "Hello, this is Rebecca from Publisher's Warehouse. I'm trying to reach one Mr. Allister Belched. He's won a considerable sum of money, but we haven't been able to get in touch with him so that he can claim his prize." Becky nodded as she listened. "I understand. Would you happen to know of anyone who might have some idea of his whereabouts?" Becky nodded again. "Okay, thanks all the same— goodbye."

"No luck?" asked H.P.

"She seemed to have nearly forgotten that she even had a half brother." Becky stood to stretch. "I'm going to check on the others in the dining room to see if they've made any progress."

"I'll go with you," said Kate. "I want to make sure Eddie's not still eating pizza."

H.P.'s smartphone rang as Becky and Kate left the living room. He was surprised by the name on the phone's screen. "Hello, dear girl."

"Hey, old man," said Vicky. "It's really good to hear your voice. I'd heard a rumor that you were dead."

"As you can tell, reports of my death are greatly exaggerated. Who told you I was a goner?"

"The internet."

"You can't believe everything you read on the world wide web."

"Nobody calls it that anymore," Vicky replied. "I've been doing some research since I saw you last—mostly online...really going down the rabbit hole."

"Wouldn't spider hole work better, what with it being the web and all?"

"Anyway, I found some posts made by one Mr. Lead over the past week about you, claiming that your Pirate Hunter stories were plagiarized. At first, I thought it was just a rehash of what happened on campus with your colleague, Fixer, a couple of years back. You know how stories on the net never die, they just get recycled."

"It's been years since I've heard anyone use the term 'net,' " said H.P.

"But it turns out this Lead character claims you ripped off accounts of his grandfather's life, who apparently really was in the Coast Guard. Then his most recent, rather ominous post—if I interpreted the emojis correctly—seems to indicate that he'd gotten his revenge by killing you in an explosion...and then I saw a press release that there in fact a fire at your friend Weston's place, which the police are being cagey about with the details for some reason."

"Vicky, I appreciate your concern, but there's no need to worry. Mr. Lead is the one who's dead…died last week in a car crash. An impostor has taken over his social media accounts and attempted to murder me and my friends, but we're all safe, staying at this farmhouse out in the middle of nowhere while the authorities hunt him down—that's why the police haven't confirmed or denied that we were killed or that the real Mr. Lead was in the car. They're waiting for this other fellow to make the next move."

"Who is he?"

"Are you asking as a friend or a reporter?"

"As someone who cares about you—dummy," Vicky answered.

"Remember us telling you about Allison Belched…it's her brother."

"Holy shit."

"You can say that again. Apparently, after doing away with us, his plan is to take down the association that his sister worked for, so as far as he's concerned, his undertaking is only half done, and frankly I wish him luck with the other half."

"Holy shit," Vicky reiterated.

Chapter 36

From the small desk in his motel room, Allister piloted the unmanned aerial vehicle on loan from the association. The military-grade UAV the coordinator lent him had a longer range and a higher service ceiling than a commercial quadcopter, though the day's overcast conditions meant he had to fly low enough to stay under the cloud base; however, the drone offered other capabilities beyond mere surveillance.

Allister had tracked Mayor McCormick's comings and goings around town for the better part of the day, but the mayor's final destination of the afternoon, before the rain began, was the town square, where it appeared preparations were underway for some sort of festival. Allister minimized the window displaying the drone's live feed on his laptop and pulled up a website sponsored by the local chamber of commerce, hurriedly reading the top story about the imminent May Day celebration. Allister grinned. He'd planned to eliminate the mayor before the weekend, but the festival offered the perfect venue for an assassination. *The headline almost writes itself: May Day Becomes Mayday!*

While tracking the mayor shaking hands and patting backs in the town square, Allister noticed a number of out-of-towners mixed in with the locals entering and exiting the downtown shops—athletic-looking men and women wearing windbreakers and sunglasses. *Feds, the perfect audience for what I have planned.*

Allister entered the command on his computer to recall the drone as the rain picked up and everyone, including the mayor, took cover inside. He'd been a little surprised that the atmosphere in the town square had seemed so convivial—at least from above. He'd figured a small town that had just lost a few of its own might blend in some mourning ribbons with all the banners and bunting. *Perhaps this community isn't as tightly knit as all that.* He glanced again at the local stories on the website—something seemed amiss.

With all his spying and traveling of the past few days, Allister hadn't spent much time online beyond making a few scurrilous posts about H.P. through Mr. Lead's social media channels to keep up appearances in case the coordinator was still keeping tabs on him. He checked his go-to news outlets for any updates about Weston and the others. *It doesn't surprise me that the police still haven't identified Mr. Lead's body from the car fire, but given that the explosion in the storm shelter occurred at Weston's home and he's unaccounted for, it is surprising that some sort of statement hasn't been issued yet.*

Allister rubbed his chin as he opened a blog he'd bookmarked. *The Donato Record* had a new post whose title he found most intriguing: Libelous Accusations Being Made By Impostor. *Not very objective to assume that claims of plagiarism leveled at your former colleague are being made by an impostor. Where's your journalistic integrity?*

Allister clicked on the link at the end of the post and watched the short segment that had aired an hour before on the cable news program that employed Vicky Donato.

There was nothing revelatory about the talking-head piece that featured a generic over-the-shoulder graphic of a car crash rather than an on-location shot; however, what caught Allister's attention was the end of the video: "An unconfirmed source states that Mr. Lead, who has seemingly spent the past several days issuing muckraking social media posts, was the sole occupant of the vehicle that exploded a week ago in the small Midwest town that has since been rocked by another explosion, though the details of that report have yet to be substantiated."

Allister closed his laptop. The phrase "unconfirmed source" played over and over in his head. *If the police knew that Mr. Lead was in the car, why wouldn't they release a statement,* he wondered, *and if they were keeping his identity a secret, why would they ever tell an out-of-town reporter?*

Then he pondered the phrase "yet to be substantiated." *What's keeping them from substantiating the details of the explosion, or at the very least acknowledging the passing of a local quasi-celebrity?*

Allister detested unknowns surfacing in the midst of a mission. He stared up at the water-stained ceiling to collect his thoughts. Then he snapped out of his pensiveness as fast as a lightbulb turning on. He quickly reopened his laptop to review the drone video from earlier in the day when the busy mayor had taken a long drive out to an isolated farmhouse. Allister paused the playback and zoomed in on Mayor McCormick emerging from his sedan—counting one, two, three pizza boxes. *Why would he deliver so much food to a house with no cars parked in the driveway?*

Chapter 37

Weston sat in a rocking chair on the veranda, listening to the light rain tapping against the top of the porch roof. He heard the screen door and turned, expecting to see Becky, but it was Slim with Gus in tow. Slim handed him a bottle of beer and sat on a nearby bench where Gus curled up at his feet, waiting impatiently to be petted.

"It was coming down in buckets there for a while," said Slim. "I was a little worried we might have us a for-real tornado, but now it's kinda peaceful."

Weston twisted the cap off his beer. "When I told people I was planning to move to a Podunk town, they'd ask how I could give up the nightlife in the city, but these days I can't imagine many better ways to spend an evening than sitting outside on a quiet night like this."

"We get plenty of those around here." Slim took a swig from his beer. "So what's eating you? I noticed you didn't have no supper."

"I guess I didn't have a taste for venison stew."

"I think Ed ate up all the veggie pizza, but I believe there's still a few slices of pepperoni in the fridge."

"I can't eat the same thing for dinner that I had for lunch. Even in college, I had to alternate between hotdogs and grilled cheese…spaghetti when I cooked for a date."

Slim stroked the fur between Gus' ears. "You should

get yourself a dog."

"Why's that?"

"Because I asked what's eating you, and you told me about what you ate back in college. I reckon you don't want to tell me what's on your mind, but you can tell things to a dog that you can't tell to people."

"Like what?"

Slim grinned. "I can't tell you."

Weston sipped his beer. "This guy's a ghost. We spent the whole afternoon calling everyone under the sun who could help us find Allister and came up with exactly nothing. He could strike at anytime from anywhere, and unless we throw a fake funeral and move to a foreign country, it's not going to take him long to figure out that he didn't succeed in killing us, at which point he's going to redouble his efforts. I've tried to put on a brave face throughout all this for Becca's sake…or maybe for mine, but the truth is that this has been going on for two years now, and I'm tired…and scared it's never going to end until it finally ends me. I'm not ready to lose my family; I feel like I just found them."

"Ain't no shame in being scared…you can use it to keep you sharp." Slim leaned back on the bench against the porch railing, staring up at the firmament. "The sky's starting to clear some…can even see a few stars through the rainclouds. I like to fly on nights like this. The sound of the soft rain falling on the wings makes you feel lonesome but also connected, know what I mean?"

"The rain falls on the just and the unjust alike." Weston took another sip of beer. "Maybe if we can't track down Allister, we can keep busy tomorrow by making a few phone calls to find the mayor's missing maypole."

Slim sat up. "Shoot—I know right where that is…at the bottom of the lake. They store the maypole along with the town's Christmas decorations down at the station—couple of new fellas on the force thought it'd be a real cute idea to take it logrolling over the summer. Them idgets didn't realize it was made from the trunk of an ironwood tree. Damn thing sank like a stone."

Weston laughed so hard he thought beer might come out of his nose.

"Hey, that reminds me—being a pilot, I always wondered what saying mayday when a plane's about to go down has to do with May Day?"

"Nothing. May Day, the spring festival, comes from England. The word *Mayday* comes from the French term M'aidez, which translates as 'help me.' " Weston watched Slim rub Gus' belly for a moment. "You already knew that, didn't you?"

"Yeah, but I bet you feel a bit better now that you had a chance to show off how smart you is."

Chapter 38

Edwin and H.P. sat reading on the farmhouse's veranda. Edwin looked at his wristwatch. "It's almost noon. I wonder what the mayor is going to bring us for lunch today?"

"Probably either Ethiopian food or sushi," answered H.P.

"You really think so?"

"No, I was being sarcastic. He brought pizza yesterday, so I'm guessing it'll be fried chicken today. If we have to stay out here much longer, he's going to run out of takeout restaurants in town from which to procure us lunch."

"Do you think the mayor remembers that I don't eat meat?"

"Yes, I'm sure he'll bring you extra mashed potatoes or whatever."

Edwin checked the time again. "I hope he shows soon...it's nearly twelve o'clock."

"So you mentioned only a moment ago." H.P. eyed Edwin's wristwatch. "I thought you swore off ever wearing a watch again."

"I did, but then I discovered how integral it is to keeping my pants zipped up."

"Sure, I'll go ahead and ask...what now?"

Edwin stood with his hands down at his side, then slowly raised his wristwatch. "I use it to verify, inconspicuously, that my fly isn't unzipped. I simply hold my wrist in front of me at the waist and then look down toward my watch to ostensibly check the time; however, usually—unless it happens to be near a mealtime—I'm really checking if my barn door, by which I mean zipper, is open. I've found it's better than looking directly at my crotch in public…Kate believes I'm making progress."

H.P. nodded. "I think she might be right."

Slim stepped out onto the veranda. "Spotted the mayor's car yet? My money's on fried chicken for lunch."

Edwin retook his seat. "H.P. is in accord with you on that point, young man, though I'm holding out hope for something with tofu."

Slim shook his head. "Not much chance of finding that in town."

"Curious," said Edwin. "One would think with so many fields growing soybeans in this agrarian community that tofu would rival corn in popularity."

H.P. rolled his eyes. "Where's Gus? I heard him barking about an hour ago, but I haven't seen him since breakfast."

"He's a farm dog," Slim replied, "so he's probably out chasing after some critter or varmint, but he's bound to show up around suppertime."

Edwin pointed down the road. "Here comes the mayor's car now."

Weston opened the screen door. "Did I hear that the mayor's on his way? I wager he's bringing fried chicken for lunch."

"That seems to be the consensus," said H.P. "Where are the ladies?"

"They went hunting for morel mushrooms in the backwoods a couple hours ago," Weston answered. "Becca thought they'd be easier to spot after last night's rain, but I think she and Kate just needed an excuse to take a break from all our testosterone."

The four watched as Mayor McCormick pulled into the driveway. He parked and exited his sedan with a striped bucket and a paper sack. "You boys look hungry."

Edwin, about to respond, paused when he heard a buzzing noise that sounded as if a swarm of locusts was hovering nearby. Mayor McCormick looked up and nearly dropped the bucket of chicken. Above his car a quadcopter descended below the roofline of the veranda so that the four standing on the porch could see it—and be seen by it. Slim ducked inside and quickly reemerged with a shotgun, firing both barrels, blasting the drone to pieces. The largest piece landed on the mayor's car, cracking its windshield.

Mayor McCormick cautiously approached his car. "What the hell is that thing?"

"Some kinda unmanned spy copter, I bet," answered Slim.

Mayor McCormick wiped drone detritus off the hood of his car. "You'd better get the gals and come with me. I don't think it's safe out here for you all anymore."

A small orange cube amid the wreckage of the UAV caught H.P.'s attention. "No, you'd better come up here with us—now!"

The Semtex exploded as Mayor McCormick finished climbing the front stairs. The blast knocked everyone to the floor of the porch and made a fiery mess of the mayor's car. As the group gathered their wits and regained their feet, Allister ambled around the side of the house holding an assault rifle at the ready. "I'm pleased you finally arrived, Mr. Mayor. I've been waiting for the past hour out in the barn for you to show. Sorry, by the way, to whosever dog that was. I'm loath to kill canines—humans I have less compunction about…especially when they're already supposed to be dead."

****

Kate knelt to examine a few mushrooms growing near the base of an oak tree. "Are these morels?"

Becky came over to inspect. "Yep, you're getting the hang of this." She opened the blade of a folding knife she'd borrowed from her husband and cut the stems of the mushrooms, placing them in an onion bag with several others they'd collected. "We'll sauté these in some olive oil for dinner."

"That sounds tasty…and it'll be good for Eddie to eat something besides potato chips and peanuts."

"I found peanut shells all over the house for weeks after Ed stayed with us when his telescope blew up."

Kate sighed as they continued their walk through the woods. "He's not the tidiest of eaters."

"It seems like you've managed to civilize him a great deal in a short time."

"If only I could convince him to get a cellphone."

"Now that you're back from your honeymoon, are you still planning to buy a new car?"

Kate nodded. "I turned in my lease just before we left, so we'll need something soon."

"Maybe consider one that has an app to remote start it and whatnot—could be enough to entice Ed to get a smartphone."

"That's a clever ploy…it just might work."

Becky smiled. "Men are like children—sometimes you have to trick them with toys to get them to do what you want."

The two stopped statue still when they heard the report of a shotgun.

"That sounded like it came from a double barrel," said Becky. "Like the kind hanging over the fireplace."

When next they heard the Semtex explode, the two set off at a run toward the farmhouse.

****

Having tied the five men to the front porch railing, Allister returned from searching the house for Becky and Kate. "I checked under all the beds and looked in all the closets…where are those two women who were with you that night you all ran out to the storm shelter? I assumed they'd be here."

"You assumed wrong, Allister my boy," said Weston. "We sent them away. Women are like children—better seen than heard…often, preferably from afar. Absence makes the heart grow fonder, and all that."

Allister studied Weston's face for a moment. "I'm not sure that I believe you, but clearly they're not here now, and as far as I know, my sister never had any quarrel with them, so let's the six of us get down to business, shall we?"

"Let's shan't and say we did," Weston replied. "Your sister's quarrel was with me alone…why not let these other nobodies go?"

"Sure, if that's what you'd prefer." Allister grinned. "I apologize—it's cruel of me to tease you that way…no, you'll all share the same fate. My sister crossed paths with each of you—except you, Mr. Mayor, but I'd intended to kill you anyway. I figure a murdered politician would compel the feds in town to look even harder at who supplied the Semtex…it's a point of pride with me that I always finish what I start—a family trait, I suppose."

"If you're going to kill us anyway, why not make it sporting?" asked Weston. "Our circumstances have given you a unique opportunity that you may never get again."

"Are you about to propose the same *Dangerous Game* scenario that you did to Dr. Weize?" Allister asked. "I've read all the association reports about you, and I've learned from each of the mistakes that've been made in the past. Besides, your offer wouldn't have the same appeal for me as it did the good doctor…I've hunted plenty of men before. However, I will give you five the opportunity to decide the means of your demise. Sis had a flair for the dramatic…truth be told, I think she might've been something of a closet pyromaniac. While waiting out in that barn, it occurred to me that I could honor her wishes by burning you alive the way she intended to; however, to satisfy my own curiosity, I'd like to know how you managed to escape from that storm shelter, and I believe the gratification of the living ought to take precedence over that of the dead, don't you agree?"

The five men looked to the others they were tied to, then four looked to Weston. "I believe I speak for all of us when I say go piss up a rope."

"You sure about that?" asked Allister. "I've seen men die in all sorts of ways…trust me, a bullet to the back of the head isn't nearly so disagreeable as being burned alive."

"Trust me," replied Weston, "the only reason we won't tell you is because you want to know so much."

Allister shook his head. "Not that much—just thought it was a cute trick, is all…like something I might one day add to my repertoire."

Allister descended the front steps and set his rifle down to unlock the chain interwoven between the balusters of the porch railing, which connected the zip ties that bound each of the men's wrists. As he turned the key in the padlock, Becky—spying from around the corner of the house—seized her opportunity and grabbed the shotgun that had been thrown by the explosion to the side of the porch steps.

Becky aimed the shotgun at Allister's chest. "Stop."

Allister turned slowly to face Becky. "Tell me, do you even know how to use one of those?"

"You mean a break-action, double-barrel, 12-gauge shotgun?" asked Becky. "I've been using them to hunt pheasant since I was twelve, though I admit I prefer an over-and-under to these side-by-side models."

Allister nodded. "I'm impressed…though shooting a human is somewhat different than shooting a bird."

"I don't think so," Becky replied. "You just aim and then pull the trigger; the task is already half done. Now put your hands up and drop down to your knees."

Allister stood motionless. "When your police friend shot my drone, it sounded like a thunderstrike—even out in that barn. I think he fired both barrels, meaning you'd need to reload before you can shoot me."

"Maybe…maybe not. I suppose you've got a fifty-fifty chance. Are you willing to risk it?"

Allister eyed his rifle leaning against the porch.

"I've faced worse odds before and come out alive." He took a step toward the gun.

"This is you last warning—stop." Seeing that Allister had no intention of complying, Becky pulled the first trigger, and it clicked—then she pulled the second, but to her dismay she heard the same hollow click.

Allister knelt to pick up his rifle. "The first rule of a firefight is to be sure you have adequate ammunition...all you've got at the moment is a makeshift bludgeon."

From the other side of the house, Kate snuck up behind Allister with a canoe paddle and bashed him over the head. "An oar is pretty good for bludgeoning too."

Allister fell to the ground like an 80,000-kernel bag of seed corn, landing headfirst in an azalea bush.

"A woman after my own heart," said Edwin from the porch.

Kate smiled at her husband. "Thanks, Eddie...and nice usage of an idiomatic phrase."

"Jesus, that was tense." Becky lowered the shotgun.

"You're telling me," Slim replied. "I spotted you creeping toward that scatter-gun, and I was shaking my head, trying to let you know that I'd already fired both barrels."

"When I saw Kate sneaking up from the other direction," H.P. said, "I had to hold my breath to keep from gasping."

"During the whole standoff I felt about as useless as decaf coffee," added the mayor.

"Or an elected official of a benighted town, I imagine." Weston held up his zip-tied wrists. "How about we get out of these before Rambo regains consciousness?"

Slim nodded. "Yep, that's the first good idea you had in a long while."

Kate grabbed the rifle and finished unlocking the padlock as Becky climbed the porch steps to cut the men loose.

Freed from the railing, Slim hogtied Allister with unused zip ties from his cargo pockets and then relieved him of two knives, a pair of needle-nose pliers, and a small grenade. "Even tied up and out cold, part of me wishes Kate had opted to go upside his head with the edge of the paddle blade instead of the broadside."

Chapter 39

Slim and the police chief spoke in the driveway, out of earshot of the others milling around on the veranda.

"Chief, this Mr. Belched is a slippery cuss. Make sure when he gets to the station that he's locked up tight and kept under constant watch."

The chief nodded. "I've already given those very orders—plus I know the FBI and ATF agents in town will be keen on interrogating him. He's going to have a lot of eyes on him."

"That's good…this one makes me nervous."

"You're not usually the nervous type."

Slim shook his head. "Nope, I usually ain't."

The chief's walkie-talkie crackled. "Chief, you there? This is the desk sergeant down at the station."

The chief unclipped the handset from his belt. "We've worked together since before we both went bald. I know who you are."

"Sorry, I ain't used to you being out in the field. I got a call from Officer Young. I'll patch him through."

"Why doesn't he just use his damn radio if he wants to talk to me?" asked the chief.

"I'd better let him explain it," replied the desk sergeant.

"Chief," said Officer Young breathlessly, "he got away."

The chief spit on the ground. "What happened, and

what's your 10-20?"

"About a mile outside of town the detainee started stirring…he wriggled loose of his cuffs and kicked out the rear door window. When I pulled over, we tussled, but before I could tase him, he grabbed my sidearm—cracked me over the head real good with it, then took my radio, which is why I'm calling you on my cellphone. He drove off in my cruiser."

The chief took a deep breath. "You okay?"

"I'm bleeding a little, but I'll be all right."

"I'll have the desk sergeant dispatch another officer to your location. Did you see which direction he took off?"

"We were at an intersection, and he turned north…like maybe he's headed for the interstate."

"Or that's what he wants us to think," Slim said quietly.

"You stay put and keep pressure on that leak of yours. We'll get you checked out at the hospital…copy all that, Sergeant?"

"Roger," replied the desk sergeant.

"I'll be back to the station after I swing by the hospital—out." The chief returned the handset to his belt. "You'd better go let your people know that this thing isn't over yet. I'll stay out here with you until the transport arrives."

Slim walked reluctantly toward the porch to update the others. "Hey, y'all, the paddy wagon will be here soon to take us back into town."

"Great," said Becky, "can we have it swing by my sister's place on the way to our house and pick up the kiddos? I think they'd get a hoot out of riding in that thing."

Slim sighed. "Affirmative on picking up Kim and the kids...negatory on going to your house."

"I sense that you're about to break some bad news," said Weston.

"Yep, I'm afraid so."

Chapter 40

Weston and Becky entered the conference room where the mayor, the police chief, Slim, H.P., Edwin, and Kate were waiting.

Weston pulled out a chair for Becky. "I'm still struggling to wrap my head around the fact that the plan was to take Allister to jail and when that failed spectacularly due to police incompetence, then plan B was to bring us all to jail instead."

The chief frowned. "I assure you, Mr. Payley, that irony isn't lost on any of us."

"I'm not sure how safe I feel locked up at a police station like this," said Weston. "Haven't any of you ever seen *The Terminator*?"

"Are the kids all tucked in?" asked the mayor.

Weston nodded. "Yeah, we set up a tent in the drunk tank…like camping, except with a stainless-steel toilet."

"My sister is reading them stories now," added Becky.

"Probably nice for her to finally see where most of her ex-boyfriends usually sleep it off."

Slim scowled. "Just so you know, the preferred term these days is sobriety cell."

The chief dimmed the lights. "All right, everyone, please have a seat. We've got some video to show you."

Slim switched on a large monitor affixed to the far wall. "That drone I blasted was a military model. In addition to being capable of carrying an explosive payload that can be remotely detonated, its onboard surveillance equipment is contained within a reinforced housing, so our IT gal was able to extract some of the video it'd taken."

Weston raised his hand. "Wait…you have an IT person on staff?"

"She splits her time between here and my office," replied Mayor McCormick. "She also helps out down at the library on occasion."

The chief began playing an excerpt of a video from his laptop on the screen. "Let's focus up. Most of the video we retrieved from the drone's hard drive, which was likely fed to the pilot's computer, was of the mayor. The timestamps are primarily from yesterday; however, we did find some footage from the day before of an individual who we don't recognize, though without the piloting computer we can't access the GPS functionality." The chief paused the video and zoomed in on the unidentified person. "Have any of you seen this man before?"

The others around the table squinted at the screen. Edwin spoke first. "I don't know him from atoms."

"Eddie, the phrase is: I don't know him from Adam," said Kate, "but I don't recognize him either."

"Me neither," added H.P.

Becky and Weston both shook their heads.

The chief sighed. "That's what we sort of figured, but I thought it worth an ask."

Slim pointed to the screen. "Since we know Allister was also looking for revenge against this association that his sister worked for, our best guess is that this is one of the head honchos of that organization. This drone video is similar to the footage of the mayor…like it was tracking his movements."

"Meaning he might've been Mr. Belched's next target after me," said Mayor McCormick.

Weston crossed his arms. "Except that we don't know who he is, or where this video was taken."

"Could this video have been intended for us?" asked H.P. "It all seems rather sloppy for this footage to fall into our hands. Perhaps Allister is hoping you'll share it with the visiting government agents…along the same line of reasoning he had for targeting the mayor in the first place."

"Maybe," Slim replied, "and we've already had our federal law enforcement guests take a gander at this here video, but it don't sit right with me—us doing exactly what Allister wants."

"What I don't understand is how Allister got away," said Kate. "He still seemed mostly dazed when you put him in the back of that police car."

"He was probably playing possum," answered the chief, "appearing conscious enough not to be taken to the hospital, but out of it enough for us not to consider him an immediate threat. I'm still kicking myself for not having him transported under armed guards."

"But his handcuffs…aren't those supposed to be escape proof?" Becky asked.

"Yes and no," Slim answered. "For your average criminal they are, but remember different departments have to be able to unlock 'em when we transfer prisoners, so if somebody's familiar with the skeleton key used across most precincts—with a bit of training— it wouldn't be too difficult to jerry-rig one of their own."

"And there was a bent hatpin on the floor of the

officer's cruiser that we found abandoned at a used car lot two towns north of here," added the chief. "Likely it had been stuck in the sole of Mr. Belched's boot for just such an occasion."

Edwin stroked his chin. "What I'd like to know is how Allister knew that we were still extant."

H.P. let out a lengthy exhale. "Regrettably, I believe I can offer some illumination on that matter. After we arrived here this afternoon, I did a bit of online research, and it seems a former colleague of mine—who I had the briefest of conversations with yesterday—may've let slip a detail I mentioned in passing, which might've been enough to raise Allister's suspicions."

Weston's eyes went wide. "Let me get this straight, my daughter was almost orphaned today because you don't have sense enough not to take a call from your ex-girlfriend—the reporter."

"She was understandably concerned because she'd heard from a source of hers that I'd been killed," H.P. replied. "With everything that we've gone through these past few days, at least all of you knew that your significant others were still alive. I didn't want her to worry…and, of course, I swore her to secrecy. The only detail she shared on her blog—in an effort to defend my professional reputation—was that Mr. Lead couldn't be the one who'd made those recent defamatory social media posts about me since he died last week. That bit of information must've tipped off Allister that the police weren't releasing everything they knew, which may've been enough for him to deduce—or at least suspect—that they were also hiding the fact that we weren't dead."

Weston pounded his fist on the conference table. "Jesus, I could give a shit about your precious reputation, you—"

Becky put a hand on her husband's fist. "The important thing is that we're all okay…and I'm back with my children now."

"It's been a tough week for all of us," Kate added, "not just for those of us who're married."

Chapter 41

Weston knocked on the half-open door to the solitary confinement cell and entered. "I noticed your light was on."

H.P. sat up on his bunk and set down the pop-culture magazine he was reading. "I'm pretty sure what you have there qualifies as contraband."

Weston held up the bottle of scotch in his hand. "What are they going to do...throw us in jail?" Weston took a seat on the bunk next to H.P. and pulled two paper cups from his sweatshirt pocket. "Besides, this is on loan from the chief...had it squirreled away in a desk drawer."

"He gave it to you?"

"I didn't say that...remind me to fill this up with tea or something when we're through with it." Weston poured three fingers of scotch into both cups and handed one to H.P.

H.P. took a sip. "The chief has good taste in liquor. I think he's going to notice if we cut his scotch with apple juice or whatever."

"Then we'll just have to finish the bottle and plant the evidence at Slim's desk."

"I suppose an apology is in order for—"

"Don't fret about it," interrupted Weston. "I overreacted."

"That's what I was about to say an apology was in order for, but then you cut me off." H.P. raised his cup.

"Water under the bridge?"

"More like booze over the gums."

The two drank in silence for a moment. Weston read the label on the bottle. "Have you ever thought of writing one of those stories in which nothing much ever happens?"

"Plenty of nothing happens in our stories."

"No, I mean a manuscript that just goes on and on in which the plot is beside the point."

"I think the Russians beat us to it," replied H.P. "Even their short stories feel like sagas to me."

"Really though, surrounded as you are in your department by all those writing instructors with MFAs whose master's theses were featured in some fancy-ass literary journal or other, it never crossed your mind to write an introspective piece…a journey into the self?"

"The thought has occurred to me on occasion, but those sorts of stories always seem to be about catharsis, which I think is better experienced than described." H.P. took another sip. "Besides, there are others who are more skilled at that type of interior writing than me."

"Don't sell yourself short. Your Pirate Hunter character hasn't endured for as long as he has on his heroic exploits alone. Readers pick up your books for the adventure, but they stay with the series for the feels."

"Are you preparing to ask me to lend you money or donate a kidney?" H.P. asked dubiously.

Weston chuckled. "No, but there is a request for a favor in the offing."

"And that is…"

"I'd like you to have another chat with Vicky—give her an update on what we know."

Chapter 42

The string of motels Allister had been staying at were starting to run together in his mind—mismatched furniture decades out of style, comforters with busy patterns to camouflage copious stains, curtains and lampshades discolored by cigarette smoke despite signage touting non-smoking ordinances—rooms adjoined by despair and distinct only in the items left by previous lodgers, such as an unmated sock under the bed or an orphaned comb behind the sink. Once Allister had discovered a diary in a nightstand drawer. He'd perused its pages but found the writing banal; he thought perhaps the author had intentionally abandoned it in hopes of making a clean break so as to begin life anew.

Allister opened the laptop that he'd chanced to retrieve from his last motel room and searched for news—if any—of the incident twenty-four hours ago at the farmhouse. The headline of the latest blog post on *The Donato Record* caught his attention, specifically the haphazard italics: *All Is Ter*minal for *Bel*eaguered *Che*erleaders.

Allister read through the blog entry detailing the plight of a cheer squad stranded in an overseas airport due to a passport mishap. The plucky cheerleaders kept up their morale by performing for travelers toing and froing along the concourse.

Allister transcribed the seemingly random italicized

letters onto a piece of stationary:

Allister Belched

I am doing research for an exposé on the association that your sister worked for. I propose an exchange of intel. I have some information that you may find revelatory. Meet me tomorrow at noon in the middle of the university quad.

Allister sneered. He smelled a trap. *The funny thing about traps is, they can be sprung both ways.*

Chapter 43

From a prone position atop the roof of the Student Union, Slim peered through his binoculars to scan the heart of campus, which was a welter of students egressing from brick buildings along the quadrangle. He picked up his walkie-talkie to report. "I see about a thousand students down there…and plenty of places for Allister to hide in plain sight."

"Give it a few minutes," Becky said into her walkie-talkie. "Most of those students will be in their next class or off to lunch soon."

H.P. put his feet up on the desk inside his office in the basement of the English building and eyed Weston sitting across from him in the chair next to Becky. "How does it feel not be the one with the radio?"

"I don't know why you're being so smug," replied Weston. "You don't have a walkie-talkie this time either."

H.P. interwove his fingers behind his head as he reclined. "But my office is command central, making me super integral to this escapade—whereas your presence is, well, just superfluous."

"I brought snacks…for me and Becca."

"Shush," ordered Becky. "I can't hear Slim."

"Because he's not talking." Weston turned back to H.P. "I'm not sure she's the right person to be the walkie-talkie operator."

Slim's staticky voice came over the radio again. "Okay, it's thinning out some…and I see a guy lingering smack dab in the middle of the quad."

"Is it Allister?" asked Becky.

"Hard to say," Slim answered. "He's got on a hat and sunglasses…but he looks to be about the right build."

"Okay, I'll text Vancy to have him do a flyby."

"Copy that."

Becky pulled a cellphone from her pocket and adroitly typed a text with one hand while holding the walkie-talkie with her other.

"Do you want me to hold the radio, dear?" asked Weston.

"No."

"I don't mind at all, in fact I'd—"

"Shush, I'm trying to send a text."

Weston shook his head. "With all this shushing, it's starting to sound like I brought snacks for one."

****

Allister stood in the center of the quadrangle with his hands in the pockets of his cargo pants, which made him feel conspicuous. Despite being only a few years older than most of the young people passing him on the sidewalk, he felt out of place. As he took notice of the faces of the co-eds, he couldn't help but think that maybe he'd missed out on something by going straight into the Army after high school, but he'd decided long ago that college wasn't for him.

Allister pressed a button on the remote concealed in his pocket. The camera he'd mounted before dawn near the top of the belltower at the end of the quadrangle panned across the roofline of the nearby campus

155

buildings. In the tiny display on the left lens of his sunglasses, he observed a lone figure atop the roof of the Student Union. He pressed another button and the camera zoomed in. *Hello, Officer.*

Vance bumped into Allister hard, knocking the sunglasses to the ground. Vance picked them up and handed them back to Allister, pretending not to notice the LCD lens. "My bad, man. I should pay more attention to where I'm walking."

Allister's first instinct was to throttle the teenager, but he quickly thought better of it and only frowned instead. "Yes, you most certainly should."

"All these girls, man...got me looking every which way but forward—you feel me?"

Allister redonned his glasses. "It is a target-rich environment."

"You got that right, ace...good luck on your finals—peace."

****

Becky depressed the talk button on her radio. "Slim, Vancy just called to confirm that it has to be Allister...says he sounded sort of military like."

"Affirmative," Slim replied. "Your boy damn near knocked him over...glad he didn't try that stunt in a dark alley."

"The little twerp—he left that part out of his report. I told him to be careful and just walk past. He did say that Allister's sunglasses had a tiny video screen inside like maybe he's watching a camera set up someplace."

"Shoot...I should've figured. Allister's probably got himself an eye in the sky. I thought it seemed a might cloudy for shades. I'll let the officers stationed at each corner of the quad know to keep out of sight, but even if

Allister does have eyes on me up here, I don't see no reason not to let Ms. Vicky go through with the exchange. He ain't stupid enough to try something with all these people around, and he can't go nowhere without a blue tail following him."

"Okay," said Becky, "we'll let Vicky know."

"10-4."

Weston reached for the radio. "Let me reply 'Buck Rogers that.' "

"Hush up." Becky turned from her husband to H.P. "You can tell Vicky we've got the green light."

"Sure thing." H.P. picked up his cellphone off the desk and made the call. "You're a go to make the exchange…but be careful, dear girl. Don't forget to wave your arm over your head if there's any sign of trouble."

****

Allister saw a familiar face approaching from the Student Union. He recognized Vicky Donato from the profile picture on her blog. He thought the trench coat she wore was a bit much.

"Who are you trying to be?" Allister asked as she drew near. "Humphrey Bogart?"

"I'm surprised you even know who that is," Vicky replied. "You look to be about the same age as the students I once taught here."

Allister pulled a binder from under his jacket and handed it to her. "When you read these association reports, it'll be you who gets the education. I want to see these posted on your blog by the end of the day."

Vicky accepted the binder. "If I think they're worthwhile, they will be."

"Now what do you have for me that's so important we had to do this in person rather than just exchanging emails?"

Vicky pulled a scrapbook from inside her coat and gave it to Allister in return. "I got this from your half sister very recently. She wanted me to have it in case I was ever able to track you down so that I could give it to you. Your mother started putting this together after she found out your sister had passed…was working on it when she died herself. It has some nice snapshots of you and Allison as children. I thought it might be worth remembering that there was more to her—and you, I imagine—than just being a cold-blooded killer…but who knows, maybe your kindergarten fingerprints will come in handy when you're arrested."

Allister grinned as he tucked the scrapbook under his jacket. "Thank you, Ms. Donato. I'm not the sentimental type, but I appreciate you bringing it to me."

"Sure thing…perhaps prison will afford you the time you need to fully appreciate it."

Vicky continued on down the sidewalk as Allister remained standing in the middle of the quadrangle.

****

"The exchange has been made," Slim said through the walkie-talkie.

Becky raised the radio to her mouth. "Where are they now?"

"It's the damnedest thing…Ms. Vicky has walked off, but Allister is still there—as if he's waiting to meet somebody else."

"Maybe he spotted your officers with his camera."

"Could be," Slim replied, "but it's awful peculiar for him to stand there like he's invisible so long as he doesn't move. Hang on—Ms. Vicky just gave the trouble signal, waving her arm real frantic like."

H.P. sat up in his chair. "What's the problem?"

"What's the problem?" Becky repeated.

"I can't say for sure," Slim answered. "She's about forty or so yards away from Allister—nearly to the edge of the quad. She's motioning toward an area between a couple of buildings. From this angle, I can't see what she's seeing."

"Is Vicky okay?" asked H.P.

"Does she appear to be okay?" Becky asked.

"She seems fine," answered Slim, "aside from waving her dang arm around. Whoa…what in the hell?"

"What?" asked Weston.

"What is it?" asked Becky into the radio.

"A whole posse of boisterous students just came out from between the two buildings," said Slim. "They're racing out toward the center of the quad…all of them got orange and blue dyed hair, and each is wearing an 'I' shirt—there's dozens of them."

"What are they doing?" Becky asked.

"Just hootin' and hollerin', being real rambunctious like," replied Slim. "Crap—Allister just took off his hat and jacket. He's got on the same 'I' shirt and hair dyed to match. They're all around him now and running toward the other side of the quad. Shit on a stick…he's in the wind—gone with the whole lot of 'em."

Chapter 44

Vicky and Vance crowded into H.P.'s subterranean office along with Weston and Becky. Slim stepped into the office, having ended his call out in the hallway. "I just got off the horn with the commissioner of the campus police. They corralled all them rowdy young fellas with the dyed hair over by the bookstore, but Allister wasn't mixed in with 'em."

"Probably slipped out just before the cops caught up to the flash mob," said Weston.

Slim pocketed his cellphone. "I reckon so. The commish told me that the group consisted of students from three different fraternities, each of which received an email yesterday from somebody posing as a former fraternity brother who wired a not insubstantial sum of money to their discretionary house fund—that is to say, beer fund—to pay for their participation in these here shenanigans today, which them boys were led to believe was a university-sanctioned event to promote school spirit."

"And none of them recognized a stranger in their midst?" asked Becky.

Vance shook his head. "There's lots of frats on campus."

"That's true," added H.P. "Each of the three houses probably didn't recognize most of the members from the other two...rather ingenious to enlist multiple fraternities like that."

"The commish had that same thought," Slim said. "He cut all them boys loose since they weren't really guilty of anything more than disturbing the peace."

Weston noticed Vicky flipping through a binder. "Is that what Allister gave you...what's in it?"

Vicky glanced up. "Reports written by various associates...your name features quite prominently."

H.P. rose from his desk chair for a closer inspection. "Like mission reports—from the field...submitted to the association?"

Vicky nodded. "It appears so."

H.P. looked over her shoulder. "That could prove invaluable for building a case against the association."

"Possibly, though hardly an ironclad case," Vicky replied. "Aside from the fancy binding, there's nothing to indicate that these documents are legitimate...they could've been typed by Allister himself—or anyone else, for that matter."

Becky sighed. "I'm still a little surprised that Allister actually showed. I mean what could he have thought you had to give him that he was willing to risk being out in the open like that?"

"That's a real good question," said Slim, "and we've set up just the place for y'all to cogitate on it, but seeing as how Allister's still in play, we need to vamoose from university grounds since it'd only take a quick looksee at the campus directory to figure out where H.P.'s office is located."

"Does that include me?" asked Vance. "I've got finals."

Slim frowned. "Allister's seen your face, but he don't know who you are, and there are forty thousand other faces for you to blend in with on campus…just promise to keep a low profile and call me at the first hint of trouble—even something small that just don't look right."

"No worries," Vance replied. "I'll keep my head down and my eyes open."

"I'm almost afraid to ask," said Vicky, "but what about me?"

"Yep," Slim answered, "it seems Allister knows all about you and your…affiliations, so you'd better come along with us to the safe house."

"A safe house, huh?" asked Weston. "Did we outstay our welcome at the station?"

Slim grinned. "We figured you'd all be more comfortable sleeping in a proper house instead of jail cells—Kim and the kids will join you tonight, and I got word a few minutes ago that Kate and Ed just arrived…but now that you mention it, my chief didn't take too kindly to the pilfering of the contents of a certain desk drawer."

Chapter 45

The coordinator leaned forward at his desk, still trying to process all the bad news he'd been given by his personal assistant. "So he lied…about everything."

The neckless PA nodded. "Our intel shows that Allister Belched had fallen off the radar since leaving the service—that is until he began posing as Mr. Lead."

"Then his story of wanting to avenge his grandfather was completely fabricated?"

"It appears so. The real Mr. Lead, in addition to being an elite member of the Coast Guard, was an avid online gamer and an ardent conspiracy theorist, but he didn't start espousing vitriol against H.P. until after he went AWOL. It's possible that Mr. Lead didn't even know of the connection between the author and his grandfather."

The coordinator sat up. "He seemed so…earnest."

"Evidently Mr. Belched is quite a capable liar…and, of course, the best lies have a kernel of truth to them. After all, he seemingly orchestrated all this to avenge a family member, so it wouldn't have taken much for him to sound persuasive about his motives."

"And I gave him the very reports that detailed his sister's termination on my orders."

"You didn't know—"

"But I should have," interrupted the coordinator.

"As you recall, I had him—or rather Mr. Lead—

vetted prior to your first meeting…before the Coast Guard had released his service status as AWOL. Then, for reasons that still aren't clear, the police suppressed the identity of the fatality of that car crash he was involved in…though I suspect Mr. Lead had been killed long before. Mr. Belched had both time and luck on his side."

The coordinator stood from his desk. "Now his time is up, and his luck is about to run out."

"I have a short list of associates within a day's drive who we could pull off assignment to—"

"No." The coordinator pointed emphatically at the chair in which his PA was seated. "That man sat in that chair and lied to my face. I take that personally…so I'm going to take care of him personally."

"The most recent information we have from our law enforcement sources place him in the vicinity of the local university…that was over an hour ago. He could be out of the state by now."

"I doubt it…he's just like his sister—a deceptive operator who doesn't know when to stand down."

"So you think he's still in the area?" asked the PA.

"He won't stray far from his quarry…I'd stake my life on it—and yours for that matter. Pack some gear. We're going on a road trip."

"How will we find him?"

"I made a foolish mistake by trusting him…but I'm not so big a fool as to ever trust anyone completely."

Chapter 46

Weston read through the association binder as H.P. sat across from him at the safe house's dining room table reading an out-of-date magazine.

Weston peered over the top of the binder. "You should put that down and read some of these reports. A few associates had some choice things to say about you."

"Like what?" asked Kate, entering from the kitchen.

"Apparently the two henchmen who kidnapped you went through H.P.'s mail when they abducted Ed and were amused by the fact that—and I quote: 'The primary resident is a subscriber of the periodical *Good Housekeeping*, though judging by the unkept condition of the residence itself, not a subscriber of its tenets.' "

Kate grinned. "That's rather droll for a henchman."

Weston turned the page. "Yes, I thought so."

"Thought so what?" asked Vicky, entering from the living room.

"We were just inquiring about H.P.'s subscription to *Good Housekeeping*," Weston answered.

Vicky nodded. "Right, I always thought that was weird…especially given that his house is usually in such shambles."

"Whose house is in shambles?" asked Becky, entering from the back porch.

"H.P.'s," answered Weston, "and yet I've just discovered that he's a subscriber of *Good Housekeeping*, which seems to me the very quintessence of irony. What say you, sir?"

H.P. sighed. "Firstly, I say that you're the quintessence of jackassedness...secondly, I say that it's none of your damn business, and lastly—if you must know—I've long had a complimentary subscription to *Good Housekeeping* because they published a short story of mine some years ago."

Becky turned to her husband. "Have you ever had a piece published in *Good Housekeeping*?"

"No," he answered, "my pieces are too dirty."

Vicky sat down at the dining room table. "Allister told me he wanted those reports posted on my blog by the end of today, but I'm not sure what that will accomplish."

"I'm not sure what any of it will accomplish," said Kate. "We have the shared goal of wanting to see the association undone; however, all we've got are grainy drone videos of the association's presumed mastermind and reports written by a few putative associates...each of whom is now dead."

Becky shook her head. "Maybe we're missing something...perhaps if we divvy up the pages in that binder and go through them together, comparing notes along the way, we'll find something more tangible that we can use."

"Disaggregating those reports seems like a good plan to me," Kate replied.

"Many eyes make for light reading," quipped Weston.

"Besides, what else have we got to do?" asked Vicky.

"I suppose we could settle on the sleeping

arrangements for tonight," offered H.P.

Vicky smiled. "Down boy."

Weston pulled at the comb binding holding the reports together. "This thing is really stuck together."

H.P. reached across the table with his keyring in hand. "While you pull, I'll use my house key to try to pry the binding loose."

After much straining by the two, the binding popped off, sending pages flying all over the dining table and revealing a flat rectangular device fastened to the inside of the metal binding.

Weston picked up the small object to inspect it more closely. "What is this?"

"It looks like a tracker," answered H.P. "We'd better let Slim know."

****

Weston, Becky, H.P., Vicky, Edwin, and Kate sat silently about the living room as they watched Slim pace back and forth while talking on his cellphone. "Okay, chief, we're leaving ASAP." Slim pocketed his phone.

"What's the word?" Weston asked.

"Kim and the kids are safe," Slim answered. "They were in transit, but the officer driving them here has been rerouted back to the station, which is where we're headed now, so gather up your things and let's get a move on."

"What about Allister?" asked H.P.

"We'll leave that tracking device behind and have a few officers stay here overnight posing as all of you. With any luck, he'll make his play soon, and they'll catch him in the act."

Becky studied her longtime friend. "It sounds like everything is under control…so why do you look so concerned?"

Slim exhaled slowly. "The circle is getting too big for my comfort level. We were able to keep the identity of Mr. Lead quiet for a while, but I think it's safe to say that cat's outta the bag. Likewise, we kept the name Allister Belched contained within my department for a bit, though now with the campus police and other law enforcement groups on his trail...well, frankly I'm worried—what with the informants an outfit such as this association is bound to have—they've become aware that Allister bamboozled them."

"So then won't they go after Allister?" asked Kate. "Maybe even make things easier for us?"

Slim shook his head. "I don't reckon it'd be that simple. The association probably figures now—and rightly so—that Allister's plan all along was to burn them, so they're likely to be of a mind to fight fire with fire...I'm afraid we might be looking at a sort of scorched-earth type scenario."

Vicky crossed her arms. "You mean to save themselves you think the association will send their people to take out Allister and anyone who's come in contact with him?"

Slim nodded. "I think that's a fair assumption."

Edwin raised his hand. "For my own clarification, in this context 'take out' means to exterminate, correct?"

Kate tenderly grasped her husband's hand and lowered it. "Yes, Eddie."

"Let's not get too far ahead of ourselves here," Slim said. "Right now, the first order of business is getting y'all back to the station. We know we can keep you safe there."

Weston stood from the couch. "But how long are we going to need to stay there? Will I have to teach my daughter to ride a bike in your impound lot out back?"

"I wouldn't worry too much about that," H.P. replied. "I imagine you can lounge in a lawn chair, offering vague words of encouragement whilst drinking a beer as easily in your driveway as you could in a cop lot."

Chapter 47

Slim navigated the unmarked police panel van through the residential neighborhood. Weston rode in the passenger's seat with the others buckled into the rear two rows of seating.

"Lots of cars parked along the street," Weston said quietly.

Slim nodded. "Yep, keep your eyes open to see if any of them start following us. I wish we'd had time to wait for an escort…for that matter, I wish we hadn't let you all leave the station in the first place."

"Hold up—the lights of that sedan we just passed on my side came on…and it's headed this direction."

"Don't get too excited yet," Slim said sotto voce. "It's a one-way street…let's just see how many turns they make with us."

"Once is happenstance. Twice is coincidence. Three times is enemy action."

"Did you write that?"

"No," Weston answered, "Ian Fleming did."

"I thought that sounded a little too good to be from one of your books."

Weston was about to rejoin when he noticed the headlights disappear from the sideview mirror. "The car turned."

"Yeah, I saw, but we ain't out of the woods yet. I'll feel a whole lot better when we get onto the interstate where the sightlines are better."

"Wouldn't it be more dangerous if Allister decided to ram us at highway speeds?"

"If I can see him coming and have some room to maneuver, I don't reckon he'd get the opportunity. Besides, when you plow into another vehicle doing seventy miles an hour, you don't tend to walk away from the crash as pretty as you please, which should count for enough to take the wind out of his sails for a freeway collision."

Weston pointed toward the windshield. "Someone's pulling out in front of us."

"I got eyes. They're probably just in a hurry. We ain't exactly burning rubber here...trying to keep a low profile and all."

"I'm just a little edgy, I guess...seeing bogeymen behind every steering wheel."

"Back in basic my drill instructor always told us to use the edginess to keep our edge—not lose our heads."

Weston sat back. "I'm not sure that makes any actual sense."

"Maybe—maybe not...the sarge was kind of an idiot, but he turned a group of undisciplined teenagers into a platoon of competent soldiers."

"No mean feat, I'm sure."

"I don't know about—"

The impact of a tow truck broadsiding the van cut Slim's response short.

Chapter 48

The cargo within secured, Allister moved quickly to affix the tow hook to the frame of the van. As he operated the levers near the passenger's side door of the truck to lift the front wheels of the van from the pavement, he spotted an inquisitive resident approaching from a house across the street.

A man in flannel pajamas eyed the van's caved-in driver's side door. "That was quite a crash…heard it over my TV with the surround sound cranked up."

With one hand on a lever, Allister used his other to grip the pistol tucked into his waistband. "Hit and run…the damage looks worse than it is."

"I don't see how that's possible. This thing looks like it was T-boned by a tank…anybody hurt?"

"No, the van's driver has already been picked up—just cuts and bruises."

"Thank a lucky star for that." As the man took a step forward to look through the broken window, his slippers crunched glass on the blacktop. "Are you going to have a crew come and clean all this glass up before morning? We've got a lot of kids in this neighborhood who like to play hockey in the street."

"They're already on the way," Allister answered.

"Great…how about the police? Should I call them? They should be notified of a hit and run."

"The driver is enroute to the police station now to

fill out a report."

"I hope they catch the guy. Shouldn't the cops dispatch an investigator to take pictures of the crime scene before you haul off this wreck?"

"The driver was able to write down the license plate number," answered Allister, "and I snapped a few photos when I first got here."

The neighbor nodded. "Full-service towing…very nice."

"As you might imagine, I've seen a lot of these types of situations, and I'm confident that this time the perpetrator will be apprehended and brought to justice."

"Good…I'd hate to think that there's some maniac out there driving amok."

The front of the van fully raised, Allister took his hand off the lever, bringing a stop to the hydraulic whine. "I'll inform the police that if they need any further information, they can knock on your door."

"Absolutely. I've got one of those doorbell cameras, and I'm always willing to do my part."

"Excellent—would you mind going back home now and reviewing the video to see if there's a good angle of the collision that might aid in their investigation?"

"You bet." The neighbor moseyed toward the cab of the tow truck. "Looks like you've got a headlight out."

Allister slowly pulled his pistol, knowing that if the nosey neighbor saw the damage to the front of the truck, the ruse would be up. "Yeah, it just blinked out on my way over here."

The two men heard something kick within the van. The neighbor turned his attention back toward where he'd been standing. "That looks like a cargo van…what's it hauling anyways?"

From the opposite side of the tow truck, Allister walked with the man to the front of the van. "This is an animal transport for the local humane society…got a few dogs in crates back there." The two heard another, harder kick. "One of them is pretty big."

"Are they all right?"

Allister pulled open the van's sliding door, saw Edwin struggling to free himself of his duct tape bonds, and summarily tased him until his legs went limp. "They're fine…just a little wound up from the accident, but I really ought to get going so they can be checked out by the vet."

"Yeah…okay," replied the neighbor. "I'll go take a look at that video for the cops."

"We always appreciate the cooperation of concerned citizens such as yourself."

Chapter 49

Allister backed up the truck with the van still in tow to the edge of a deserted parking lot of the scenic viewpoint atop Lookout Mount. He exited the truck, walked to the split rail fence behind the van, and unfastened two of the rails from the nearest post. He assessed the opening he'd made in the fence and figured it afforded enough clearance to back the van onto to the narrow dirt area and then off the sheer precipice beyond.

Allister returned to the van and opened the sliding door. Six sets of eyes stared back at him from the bench seats. Slim still lay unconscious on the floor, having taken the brunt of the impact in the crash. "Good, I see that all but one of you is alert now. I'm sure you must still be feeling somewhat disoriented. I can relate, having recently been thumped on the head with a canoe paddle. Anyway, I'd like to take a moment to apprise you of the situation so that you're aware of what's happening when it happens. It's funny, I went to all the trouble to trap you by concocting that elaborate tornado illusion, but now you've gone and trapped yourselves with very little effort on my part." Allister turned to Vicky. "I'm truly sorry that you became entangled in this…imbroglio, but if it's any consolation, you'll likely become far more famous in death than you ever would've during your career. I wanted to assassinate the mayor to bring further attention to the people I'm attempting to implicate, but I suppose snuffing a small-time reporter will be just as effective as offing a small-town politician."

Vicky squirmed against her restraints. Allister leaned into the van and removed the strip of duct tape covering her mouth. "Did you want to say something?"

"Small time? I'm national, you son of a bitch."

Allister reapplied the duct tape and looked over at H.P. "She's a feisty one, isn't she?"

H.P. shouted into the duct tape covering his mouth. Allister moved to take off his tape but then reconsidered. "Weston, before I send you and your friends careening off the side of this mini-mountain, I'll let you have the last word, since you meant so much to my sister, but I'll remind you that you'll be speaking for the entire group, so please keep in mind your circumstances before suggesting that anyone go jump off a cliff."

Weston exhaled heavily as Allister peeled away the tape from his mouth. "If I wasn't certain it'd be a complete waste of breath, I'd tell you again to let my friends go and exact your revenge on exactly who deserves it—me, but I know it'd require someone with more brains and class than you to honor such a reasonable request."

"I find your gallantry both touching and moving." Allister's lips twisted into a smirk. "So much so that now I intend to touch the tow truck's gear shifter to move this van right over the edge."

Weston shook his head. "I still can't believe we didn't expect a spineless, secreting cephalopod such as yourself to secrete that tracking device into the spine of the binder you gave us."

Allister froze in the process of closing the van door, paused for a moment, and then slid it back open. "What tracking device?"

"The tracker you hid in the crack of…" Now it was Weston's turn to smirk. "Ah, that wasn't your handiwork we found, was it?"

"In point of fact it wasn't. I've been tailing this van since I saw you all leave campus in it this afternoon." Allister's head swiveled suddenly as he noticed headlights driving up the road to the small parking lot. "That's my cue to make a tactical retreat—sorry, no more time for protracted goodbyes."

Allister slammed the sliding door shut, raced to the cab of the truck, shifted the gear selector into reverse, and then darted off into the nearby woods.

****

All was darkness again inside the van. Weston felt the vehicle creeping backwards. He knew they had only scant seconds before they'd plummet to their death. Ignoring the protests of his middle-aged joints, he tucked his knees against his chest and stretched out his arms, pulling his bound hands from behind his back and over his feet. Since the duct tape from his mouth had been removed, he was able to quickly gnaw through the tape around his wrists. His hands free, he tore away the tape binding his ankles.

Weston swiftly scrambled up the inclined floor of the van to the steering wheel and stomped hard on the brake pedal. The rear wheels of the van locked, but the mass of the tow truck continued to push the van across the ground. He shifted the gear selector into park and yanked on the emergency brake. Finally, the van came to a stop.

Weston collapsed into the driver's seat and glanced at the sideview mirror. Seeing how close the rear of the van was to the edge, he shot out of the seat and into the back of the van, throwing open the sliding door and hurriedly pushing the others onto the ground, being careful not to let them roll off the cliff.

Weston freed Becky first, and then the two set to cutting their friends loose. A police cruiser pulled into the lot and parked in front of the tow truck. An officer exited the vehicle and surveyed the scene. "What are you all doing up here?"

"Nice night for a picnic," replied Weston, gasping for breath.

"Where did you come from?" asked H.P.

"I was on my way to escort you enroute when the chief radioed that you guys were off course…by miles. Our department vehicles are LoJacked, you know. Anyways, I've been driving all around this area as the LoJack's signal doesn't account for elevation."

Slim moaned as he sat up.

"Slim, you okay?" asked the officer.

"I'll be okay." Slim rubbed the back of his neck as he assessed his surroundings. "But I'm not sure I want to know how we got way up here."

"By the looks of it, you were towed." The officer patted the hood of the tow truck. "We'd better shut off this wrecker before—"

The slight nudge enabled the wheels of the tow truck to once again gain purchase on the muddy ground, causing it to roll backwards just a bit. The rear wheels of the van then slipped off the edge of the cliff. All and sundry stared helplessly as the van proceeded to pull the truck straight down the side of Lookout Mount.

****

From a parked car near the base of Lookout Mount,

the coordinator trained his night-vision binoculars up at the scenic observation point, watching as the van and tow truck tumbled toward the bottom. "I don't think Mr. Belched will be coming down the same way he went up."

"Do you think he's still in the tow truck?" asked the PA from the driver's seat.

"No, I saw him get out…but now I see that cop we noticed driving around earlier peering down over the side, so I doubt he's in police custody either."

"Maybe the cop spooked him, and he ran off into the woods."

"Maybe." The coordinator depressed a button on his expensive binoculars to switch over to thermal imaging and scanned in every direction. "This area is teeming with oranges and reds among all the purples and blues."

The PA nodded. "Lots of wildlife out there."

"Good…perhaps Allister will get eaten by a bear or something, though I don't suppose I'll be satisfied unless I actually see his eviscerated carcass."

Chapter 50

Slim sat in the station's conference room with his left arm in a sling while holding an icepack with his right hand against the back of his head.

Weston entered the room. "Careful with that icepack...somebody with a brain your size is in real danger of having it freeze up and shrivel away completely. You might lose it next time you blow your nose and never even know it's gone."

Slim smiled. "The doc says I should make a full recovery in a few weeks—thanks for asking. Is everybody bunked in for the night?"

"All appear to be resting peacefully in their respective cells. Why'd you have me rousted from my slumber in the slammer?"

Slim slid an envelope across the conference table. "This was delivered twenty minutes ago to the desk sergeant by a teenager who told us he'd been paid fifty bucks to drop it off. I wanted you to have a look at it before I showed it to my chief and the others in the morning."

Weston sat down, opened the letter-sized envelope, and read the single sheet of paper it contained. "Damn...I was hoping Allister assumed we were all still in the van when Barney Fife sent it careening over the cliffside."

"No such luck...but who's Barney Fife?"

Weston squinted slightly. "You know...the cop

from that old TV show?"

"Right, the one set in New York City with Abe Pagoda as Fish…yeah, I think I remember that one."

"No, not Barney Miller—Barney Fife…Mayberry, not New York." Weston sighed. "Oh, just forget it."

"Consider it forgotten. So based on what you all told me earlier tonight, Allister's spooked now that he knows the association is on to him…seems like he's ready to wheel and deal. What do you think?"

"I say we take the deal…what other option is there?"

Slim pointed to the paper. "Another option—a better option, in my opinion—would be to ignore that completely."

"This is a good offer. If we don't take it, then the alternative—and we both know there'll be one—will likely be much, much worse."

Slim nodded. "Could be…of course we'll have you surrounded the whole time by officers who'll stay out of sight, but—"

"But we both know Allister is too clever for that."

"I gotta give it to him—he's wilier than a fox fittin' to feast in a chicken run."

"Then we'll just have to out-wily him."

"Wouldn't that be outfox?" asked Slim.

"Sure, we'll do that too." Weston refolded the letter into the envelope and slid it back to Slim. "Do me a favor though…don't mention this to Becca and the others until it's all over."

"I don't think Becky's gonna like that none."

"Hopefully I'll live to regret it."

"Okay, but if you expect me to let you go into the crosshairs like this, I want you to do me a favor in return. I got something of mine I want you to wear."

"Your badge…Slim, I'd be honored."

Slim shook his head emphatically. "Shit, I bet you would be."

Chapter 51

The police chief finished explaining with the wall map where each of the dozen officers seated in the conference room would be positioned. "Quite frankly, we're fortunate that this Belched character chose a location for the exchange with so much cover. You can tell from looking around the room that this is an all-hands-on-deck situation, but I'm confident that if each of us does his or her part, we'll be able to bring this matter to a close by the afternoon, and our town can finally get back to business as usual."

"Hear, hear," enthused Mayor McCormick.

The chief nodded reluctantly toward the mayor. "At his request—"

"And over your objection," Mayor McCormick interrupted.

"The mayor has seen fit to join me in the mobile command unit to oversee this sortie." The chief's finger swept past each of his officers in the room. "When any of you gets eyes on Mr. Belched—or anything else that appears out of place—radio in immediately…no matter how seemingly insignificant it might be. On its own, what you're seeing may not seem like a cause for concern, but remember I'll be the one looking at the big picture, and that picture will be a whole lot clearer with input from all of you. We're going to be a well-coordinated team out there, and I'm the play caller.

Await my order to interdict…no lone cowboys in this posse—understood?" The chief marked all the nodding heads of his officers. "Okay then…drive out to the site four to a cruiser. I don't want the area looking like a cop car parking lot."

A female officer raised her hand. "Chief, there's twelve of us—that means only three squad cars. Where will we put the bad guy when we catch him?"

"My vote is the coroner's van," said Weston.

Slim smiled. "We'll cross that bridge when we come to it."

"Let's just focus on apprehending Mr. Belched first," the chief added. "You all know your assignments, so get after it…and let's be careful out there."

The chief approached Slim and Weston as the officers filed out of the room. "You two sure you're up for this?"

"Absolutely," answered Slim.

"Sure thing," said Weston, "and I appreciated your *Hill Street Blues* reference."

Slim snapped his fingers. "Book 'em, Danno…right?"

Weston rolled his eyes. "You're only off by about five thousand miles."

The chief placed a hand on Weston's shoulder. "When this all goes down, it may feel like you're out there on your own, but you'll have nearly the entirety of this town's police force backing you up. We might be small, but we're mighty…and if need be, we can loop in our federal law enforcement guests, though I'd like to continue to keep them out of this unless absolutely necessary. They have a tendency to take over, and they may not approve of you being the point man for this operation."

Weston nodded. "I understand…and honestly, I don't approve of me taking point either, but I think this is our best shot of ending this once and for all."

Slim patted Weston on the back. "I gotta hand it to you…you've got stones."

"Too bad they're in my kidneys."

"Good luck, Weston," said the mayor.

"You won't see us, but we'll see you out there." The chief followed the last of his officers from the conference room with the mayor close behind.

When the doorway cleared, Weston noticed H.P. waiting out in the hallway. "Remember what I requested—that we keep this thing under our hats."

"That's why we timed this little conference to coincide with breakfast," Slim replied.

H.P. approached the pair. "If the police are really trying to keep this quiet, then they ought to invest in soundproof doors."

"How much of our surprise party plans did you overhear?" asked Weston.

"Enough to know that I disapprove of the guest list," answered H.P. "So I take it you heard from Allister."

"He sent a note late last night," Slim said. "Wants a redo of yesterday's high-noon exchange."

Weston glared at Slim. "That's not keeping this under your hat…more like wearing a neon sign over your hat."

"What's he trading this time?" asked H.P.

"Now that the association is in play, it seems Allister is anxious to wrap things up," Slim answered. "He says he'll turn over every bit of incriminating information he has about the association and leave the rest of us alone forever if old Weston here turns hisself over to him."

H.P. frowned at Weston. "And, of course, you unilaterally decided to accept the offer without consulting with the rest of us."

"A consultation didn't seem necessary given that this is the only sensible course of action," replied Weston.

"Sensible—really…since when is that what you're known for?" H.P. asked rhetorically. "I can see that it's beyond my power to talk you out of this, so I'm going with you."

"Allister warned that I have to come alone or else the deal is off," Weston said.

"Then I'm not going with you—I'm going with Slim." H.P. folded his arms. "See, I can be obstinate too. Look, you two need me. Slim's got a broken arm, and you're half stupid."

Slim sighed. "There's no arguing against facts."

Edwin entered the conference room.

"What about you?" asked Weston. "How long have you been eavesdropping?"

"Me…eavesdropping? No, I saw cops leaving here, so I came in looking for donuts that they might've left behind—breakfast this morning is heavy on the sausage."

"We're planning to go with Weston, who's foolishly decided to meet up with Allister," said H.P. "Care to tag along? Fair warning though, saying yes may endanger life and limb."

"Yes," Edwin replied without hesitation, "and let's hope it only occasions danger to the latter since I have more of those to spare."

Chapter 52

Weston walked slowly down the driveway toward the charred remains of his grandfather's house. The air was crisp. He pushed his hands into his sweatshirt pockets to keep them warm. He hadn't been back since touring the lot with his insurance agent. The lawn was overgrown, but most of the soot had been blown away, so on balance everything looked better than it did before, like nature was midway through its leisurely process of reclaiming the small patch of land he'd once known as home—ashes to ashes and dust to dust.

"Everybody's in position," Slim radioed into Weston's earpiece. "There are over a dozen sets of eyes watching out for you, and Ed's scanning the sky for more drones…not a bad guy in sight."

Weston surveyed the wooded area beyond the property line and then looked back at the woods across the road that ran in front of his erstwhile residence. The trees were so thick in every direction that he doubted a hundred cops could find a sniper who'd been trained to conceal himself in foliage. At least they'd be able to get a bead on Allister once he fired his first shot.

"Heads up," said Slim. "There's a car inbound about a half mile east of your position. The chief just gave the order to have the road team intercept."

Weston turned to his right, but he couldn't see anything beyond the bend in the road. He stepped onto the scorched slab of the house's foundation. All that remained perpendicular to the concrete was a mound of bricks that had constituted the fireplace, which were no longer in the shape of a mantel or a chimney.

"It appears the sedan has two occupants," Slim reported. "They're pulling over for the road team now."

Weston placed his heel on a friable looking brick and watched as it crumbled under his foot. *How hot must've my house burned to do this to a brick my grandad used to build a fireplace,* Weston wondered. He couldn't help thinking of Allison's half-burnt face the last time he'd seen her.

"The team says neither in the car is Allister, but at first glance the two seem like heavy hitters," Slim radioed, "not just some locals on their way to go fishing, but so far they're complying with the officers' orders."

Weston noticed a small pile of bricks set apart from the central mound. As he neared, he could see that they had been neatly stacked.

"Okay, the team has them detained for further questioning," Slim reported, "but they look the type to plead the fifth."

Weston knelt down and began to unstack the three layers of bricks.

"Yep, like I figured, they want to lawyer up," Slim said, "so we'll take them into custody until their counsel arrives."

Under the bottom layer of bricks, Weston found a white envelope.

"This is interesting," radioed Slim. "H.P. showed me a picture of the two goons the team just texted him, and the older one looks like the fella in that drone footage we saw."

Weston opened the envelope and pulled out the index card within. Flipping it over, he read the words: Who's minding the store?

Weston set off at a run.

Chapter 53

Weston and Slim entered the police station like whirlwinds. Finding the front desk unoccupied, they quickly made their way back to the cellblock. They discovered the desk sergeant locked in the first cell, his wrists bound with duct tape and another strip covering his eyes with Weston's name written across it.

"What happened, Sarge?" asked Slim.

The desk sergeant tilted his head up. "He got in somehow and set off the fire alarm. Struck me on the back of my head as I was trying to get the women and children out. I just came to a moment ago."

"We'll have you out of there in no time," said Slim.

The sergeant shook his head. "Don't worry about me—go check on the others."

Inside the first cell of the adjoining room, they found Kate and Vicky similarly bound with duct tape. The word COME written across the strip covering Kate's eyes and ALONE on Vicky's strip of tape.

"Where are the others?" asked Weston.

Kate turned her head. "In the next room…I think."

"We heard screaming," added Vicky. "Hurry."

The two entered the final room of the cellblock and heard noise coming from solitary confinement. Slim pulled open the cell door to find Lance, Kim, and Ance bound together with duct tape. On the three strips covering their eyes were written the words I, MEAN, and

IT.

"Kim, it's me," Slim said. "You're safe now."

"Where's Becca?" asked Weston.

"Allister took her," Kim answered. "He told me to tell you that he's going to finish the game the shrink started…and that you should come alone."

Weston nodded. "I got the message."

****

Slim slammed his hand down on the conference table. "No way, no how."

"It's not your call," Weston replied.

"That's true," said the police chief. "It's mine, and my answer is: no way, no how."

Weston crossed his arms. "You all were perfectly willing to let me walk out into the open, surrounded by woods in every direction. You know Allister could've taken a shot at me if he wanted to. How is this any different?"

"The difference is that we had a reasonable chance of spotting him before he could get a shot off," answered the chief. "This is letting you walk down into the lion's den alone."

"Us cops are used to taking risks," added Slim. "That's the job, but this ain't just risky—it's damn near suicide."

Mayor McCormick nodded. "I concur. I won't allow one of my citizens to forfeit his life in an effort to save another when we have no guarantee that this killer will even honor the exchange."

"In all likelihood he'd simply kill you both," said H.P.

"If he hasn't killed Becky already," Edwin added.

Kate rubbed her husband's neck to silence him.

Edwin pressed his fingertips together. "I only mean it's a possibility that we ought to consider. If this really is the deathtrap that we all believe it to be, then we have to think through every eventuality in order to arrive at the most informed decision."

"You're talking about odds and what-ifs," replied Weston. "I'm talking about my wife."

Slim raised his hand in a calming gesture. "Becky's important to all of us. I've known her since we were kids, but Kim's out in the hall now with your kids. You need to consider them too; I'm certain they'd be Becky's top priority."

"I've only known most of you a short time," said Vicky, "but the economics are pretty clear to me. Given your ages and contributions to the greater good—no offense—Becky's life has more value than yours, Weston, but you doing this would be like throwing good money after bad."

"You're saying we ought to just cut our losses?" asked Weston rhetorically. "Gee, new person, I appreciate the consult and all, but you can jam it in—"

"Whoa, we're all just thinking out loud here," interrupted the mayor, "and nobody's saying anything about cutting our losses. Chief, you must have some ideas for getting Allister out of that bunker."

The chief pointed to Slim and Weston. "After we went to that shooting club to get these two, we mapped out that underground range before we sealed it up. There's only one entrance through a narrow hallway. If I send in a phalanx of officers, Mr. Belched could mow them down without ever exposing himself from behind cover. If we try using heavy equipment to dig them out, we'd run the risk of collapsing the roof on top of them.

That main room, where the lab had once been, is so cavernous that it'd take hours to fill if we drilled holes and dropped down teargas canisters to smoke them out, completely forgoing the element of surprise to say the least. No, my best recommendation—the only strategy that makes any sense—is to do the most difficult thing of all…wait."

"Starve him out?" Weston asked incredulously. "Allister could've stockpiled months of provisions down there, which he may not feel inclined to share with Becca if he thinks he'll have to outlast a protracted siege."

The chief shook his head. "He didn't go to all this trouble just to play the waiting game. Those two persons of interest we picked up and plan to turn over to the feds appear to be members of this association. If they can positively ID the older of the two using facial recognition as the one in that drone video…well, it could go a long way toward building a Racketeer Influenced and Corrupt Organizations case against the whole lot of them. Mr. Belched knows the association is onto him now and desperately wants this guy out of the picture, which is probably why he sent him in our direction for us to collar, but he must be aware that more of these associates will come after him, and I'm sure he can feel the ground shrinking beneath his feet. No, once Mr. Belched realizes that we have no intention of turning you over to him, I think he'll bug out of his foxhole sooner than later, leaving Becky behind and unharmed, since—as Slim reported—he didn't seem too disappointed about not having captured her at the farmhouse."

Weston turned to Slim. "As far as bosses go, you've got a pretty smart one."

Slim grinned. "Don't go telling him that…wouldn't

be good for any of us."

Weston walked toward the door of the conference room. "I don't like this choice, but as you say chief, because it's hard probably means it's the right thing to do. Anyway, I need to check on the kiddos and then see a man about a horse."

Chapter 54

Weston drove the Mustang down the unpaved backroads at breakneck speeds. He knew his absence wouldn't go unnoticed for long, just like he knew he'd never be able to live with himself if he didn't do everything he could to save his wife. Soon he arrived at the mud-puddle landmark and hooked a hard right onto the grassy lane that led past the burned-out gatehouse and the graffitied mansion to an open, overgrown area that had once been a well-manicured skeet shooting range. He drove the old coupe through the tall weeds to the fringe of the wooded area where the hidden entrance to the underground bunker awaited him.

Weston killed the engine and walked purposefully into the trees, quickly finding the metal door set in the ground that led to the behemoth bunker beneath him. The padlock rested unshackled in the hasp staple. He lifted the heavy door, pulling it the full 180 degrees its hinges would allow so that it landed with a loud thud on the hardpack earth. He descended the subterranean stairs.

****

Slim stood in the conference room, consulting the wall map with the police chief. The desk sergeant entered with a wet paper towel pressed against the back of his head. The chief turned toward him. "I thought I ordered you to go to the hospital and get checked out. You need stitches."

The sergeant nodded. "I'm on my way—just wanted to make sure everybody was situated before I left. You all need anything?"

"No, Sergeant, we're fine," the chief answered. "I'll follow up with you later and inform you of any developments."

"I'd surely appreciate that...like to see the guy who did this to me behind bars for a good long while."

The chief nodded. "I'm certain we all share your hope of seeing this matter concluded with a lengthy incarceration."

Slim stood staring into the middle distance, silently hoping for a conclusion with more finality, when he noticed the water dripping from the sergeant's paper towel. "Did you get that from the washroom up front?"

The sergeant followed Slim's gaze to the drips of water on the floor. "Yeah, sorry about that. I've had my head over the sink for the last fifteen minutes. I thought it was all dripped out."

"Is Weston still in there?" asked Slim.

"No, I ain't seen him since before you all came in here," answered the sergeant.

"Maybe he went to use one of the restrooms back in the cellblock," offered the chief.

Slim shook his head. "Seems kinda unlikely that he'd go to all the trouble of passing through the security doors just to see a man about a...chief, remember that hotrod we impounded back when I got shot?"

"The Mustang?" asked the chief. "We've been holding onto that jalopy in our lot out back until the owner can come claim it after he serves a bid at county for failure to appear. You don't think by 'horse' Weston meant—"

Slim sprang for the door. "I sure as hell do."

****

Weston approached the opaque glass door at the end of the cinderblock corridor and knocked hard with his fist. The clean-room door opened just wide enough to reveal Becky with a gun held to her head.

"Did you come alone as instructed?" asked Allister from behind the door.

Weston hated to see his wife so frightened. "Yes."

"No tricks?" Allister asked.

"I'm not smart enough to trick you, Allister…just let my Becca go—that's all I want."

Allister opened the door wide and wrapped an arm around Becky's neck while still holding his pistol to her head. "And all I want is to do right by my sister; it seems we're both at the mercy of the women in our lives."

Weston tried to smile at Becky. "I was always afraid that one day I'd find you in the arms of a younger man."

"I'd give anything to be in yours right now," Becky replied.

Allister walked her into the corridor. "If your husband is true to his word, I'll give you two a moment for a final farewell."

"I appreciate that you're big on goodbyes…most of the bad guys I've encountered aren't so considerate." Weston backed up as Allister and Becky advanced. "So how's this going to go?"

"Smoothly, I anticipate," answered Allister. "I've given your wife a flash drive with a video that I've put together, which contains—among other things—the rather incriminating audio recording of the last meeting I had with the head of the association…that older fellow I tricked today into driving out to where my sister had been disfigured. I didn't have a chance to make use of the video myself, since it would seem the world now knows that Mr. Lead is dead, so it's hers to do with as she sees fit—leak it to the press, post it on social media, turn it over to the authorities…whatever, so long as it's disseminated, it'll ensure the eventual end of the association."

"Eventual?" asked Becky.

"These things take time," Allister replied, "which could spell bad news for you and me in the months ahead…that is if none of the tripwires I've set in the woods above us goes off, rendering it all a moot point. See, you're my insurance. If I'm convinced that Weston really did come alone, then I'll keep my end of the bargain and let you go, but the only way I'll be convinced is if I shoot him in broad daylight and no one tries to stop me."

"What happens if someone does?" Becky asked.

Allister pulled a grenade from his jacket pocket and held it up for her to see. "Again, you and I won't have to worry about the association getting to us before law enforcement can get to them. Now up the stairs."

****

Slim skidded his squad car onto the grassy lane. His radio squawked. "This is the chief. What's your 20?"

Slim picked up the mic. "I'm near the ranch. No sign of any runaway horses. Must've been a bogus call—over."

"Not a single stray horse outside the fence?" The chief's voice sounded skeptical, though for the moment he seemed unwillingly to ask any direct questions that would contradict Slim's flimsy cover story lest their conversation was being monitored on a police scanner.

"None that I can see." Slim followed the fresh tire tracks in the wet grass.

"I have other officers in the area out near the ranch," replied the chief. "Should I dispatch them to your location to help you search along the perimeter fence?"

"Negative…too many people might spook any horses that I do come across."

"In that case, just radio if you suddenly find yourself in a stampede, and I'll send the calvary pronto."

Slim registered the reluctance in his chief's voice to hold off on sending backup. "Copy that."

"Then happy hunting—out."

****

Weston's eyes took a moment to adjust to the daylight as he emerged first from the underground bunker. He gave half a thought to pulling his wife by the hand and making a run for it into the woods before Allister's eyes could fully adjust to the afternoon sun, but he thought better of it, figuring that Allister was likely a crack marksman under almost any circumstances and that they were surrounded by tripwires, so taking such a risk would likely only result in both of them ending up dead.

"Stop right there," ordered Allister as he and Becky took the final step up to the ground level.

Weston turned to face Allister. "Not such a bad day to die."

"I'm a little surprised by your air of…resignation," Allister said. "No appeals to my better angels or would-be witticisms about my surname?"

Weston shook his head. "No, you've won, Allister. You've given Becca the evidence needed to put the association away, so I know you'll honor our exchange—my life for hers…I'm fine with that."

"You have a very devoted husband." Allister released Becky. "Go to him and say your goodbyes."

Becky nearly fell into Weston's arms. He held her tight. "Whatever happens, it's going to be okay, Becca. You and the kids are going to be okay—that's all that matters. You've given me so much."

"We haven't had nearly enough time."

He wiped away her tears. "If we'd lived to be a hundred together, it still wouldn't have been enough time."

"Well, I imagine when you turned a hundred, she'd only be an octogenarian." Allister raised his pistol. "Sorry, just an observation…hope it didn't ruin the moment, though I suspect what comes next surely will."

Weston kissed Becky and then pushed her away.

Allister aimed. "From what I've read in the association reports, my sister's mistake when it came to you, aside from making things personal, was taking too long to shoot. She should've fired two shots right off, center mass—just like we were trained."

The couple cracks of gunfire that followed instantly sent birds aloft from the nearby tree branches. Weston, with a pair of scorch marks on his sweatshirt, reeled backwards and fell into a shallow ravine.

Allister stood above him; seeing Weston face down in the mud, he was satisfied that he'd accomplished his mission. He turned to Becky, whose stoic expression he interpreted as shock. "I regret that it had to be this way…I wish you the best with what's to come." With that Allister jogged toward the clearing beyond the trees.

Becky climbed down into the ravine, lifting her husband's head from the mud. "It's okay to breathe now."

Weston slowly opened his eyes. "I would if it didn't hurt so much."

"That was quite a performance."

"Not really…gravity did most of the work. You're the one who deserves the Oscar—not letting on that you felt the bulletproof vest when you hugged me, though I suppose what's more likely is that you assumed it was my chiseled physique."

"You can't chisel butter, dear."

The two looked up from the ravine when they heard the metallic crunching sound of a car crash. Then they instinctively covered their heads a moment later when they heard an explosion.

"What in the world was that?" asked Weston.

"Let's hope a good end to a bad situation." Becky attempted to sit Weston upright. "I'll help you get out of here."

Weston feebly waved his hands. "Let me just lay here for a minute more."

"Becky…Weston," Slim bellowed. "Can you hear me?"

Weston coughed. "So much for a respite."

"We're over here," Becky shouted.

Slim soon appeared at the top of the ravine. "Ain't the pair of you a sight…just a wallowing in the mud— like a couple of pigs, pleased as can be."

"That's rich, coming from a cop," replied Weston. "Thanks, by the way, for making me wear that vest of yours."

Slim reached down an arm to help Becky up. "I figured it might come in handy."

"What happened to Allister?" Becky asked as she

climbed out of the ravine.

"I spotted him coming out of the woods just as I drove up. He darted for the Mustang, but I rammed into him right as he began to make his getaway. My airbag deployed and his didn't."

"Those early airbags weren't designed to last thirty-plus years," Weston said, "but what was that explosion?"

"I imagine that grenade Allister was showing off," answered Becky.

Slim nodded. "Yep, Allister hobbled out of the wreck with what looked like a broken leg and probably an arm or two to boot…couldn't even level his gun in my direction. He saw that I had the drop on him, so he reached into his coat pocket. Next thing I know—boom. I reckon he figured taking his own life was better than spending the rest of it behind bars."

Weston exhaled. "You know, in a strange way, I'm glad Allister thought he succeeded in killing me…maybe it gave him some peace before he died."

"I don't know about all that, though he definitely died in pieces." Slim climbed down into the ravine. "Now let's see about getting you out of here."

"Be careful, you lanky oaf…even with this vest on, getting shot was no picnic."

"You don't have to tell me," Slim replied. "I've been shot while wearing it before, remember?"

"Sure, but just once…I survived two gunshots."

Becky rolled her eyes. "Okay, boys, you can compare bullet wounds later—right now I want to go see my kids."

Chapter 55

The police chief entered the sobriety cell to find Becky, Weston, and Lance playing Yahtzee on a small folding table. Ance sat on Weston's knee, helping him keep score.

The chief couldn't help but smile at the scene. "That's not the sort of dice game typically played in our jail."

"Ance and I are up half a dozen cigarettes," said Weston.

"From what I understand, that's enough to trade for a pudding cup," replied the chief.

Ance looked up at the chief. "Scotch?"

"You have the same taste as your daddy," the chief said.

"She's trying to say butterscotch." Lance rolled all five dice. "It's her favorite."

"Any news from the FBI?" asked Becky.

The chief nodded. "They've finished attempting to interrogate the two men we picked up earlier today, though they agree that the older one looks like the same individual in the drone footage I showed them."

" 'Looks like'?" asked Weston skeptically. "I thought the feds were going to use some fancy-ass facial recognition software?"

Lance tilted his head toward Ance. " 'Ass' as in donkey, right?"

"That's right," Weston said, "I meant fancy-donkey software."

"In due time," said the chief. "For now, the agents had to cut them loose at their attorney's insistence."

Becky's eyes went wide. "Wait, they're free to go?"

"They just left," the chief replied. "We held them as long as we could, but we can't hold them indefinitely for driving in a suspicious area and resembling someone in a drone video taken by a known criminal."

"But what about the flash drive I've got?" Becky asked.

The chief nodded again. "Yes, the agents are most anxious to see it. They're hoping it will help them with the case that they've been building for the past few months."

"Months?" Becky looked across the table at her daughter and youngest son. She pulled the flash drive from her pocket, tossed it to Weston, and bolted for the exit.

The officer at the front desk gave her a curious look as she raced out to the parking lot. She quickly found two men, one older, the other neckless, talking with a woman in an expensive suit.

"I appreciate you getting here on such short notice," said the older man to the suit.

"That's why you pay my exorbitant retainer." The woman used a key fob to unlock a German sedan parked nearby. "For today, I believe this matter is concluded, but if any of the local law enforcement should make trouble for you on the way out of town, just call me on my cell, and I'll turn right back around."

"Wait," shouted Becky. "I want to talk to you."

The neckless man took a step toward her, but the

older man put a hand on his shoulder. "What is it?"

Becky slowed to a jog and tried to catch her breath. "I'm glad I caught you…I mean, I'm glad I caught up to you—no one's caught anyone, yet."

The woman in the suit raised an eyebrow. "Are you attempting to harass my clients…in a police parking lot, no less?"

Becky shook her head. "No, sorry for running after you like this…it's just been an all-around crazy-donkey day."

"I agree with you there," said the older man. "What can I do for you?"

"I have information," Becky blurted, "given to me by Allister Belched…you know, Allison's sister."

The older man raised a finger. "I think I may know of whom you're referring, but first I need to let my attorney get on the road. We've taken up enough of her time today, and she has a long drive ahead of her."

The woman in the suit nodded hesitantly. "Yes…I suppose I should be going, but as I mentioned—call me if you need anything."

The older man waited as the lawyer got into her car. Then he turned back to Becky. "I was just informed that Mr. Belched is no longer with us. You say he gave you some information before his untimely passing?"

"His passing was timely enough for my liking." Becky exhaled. "Listen, you're the big bad…everybody knows it, and Allister worked really hard to prove it— told me he secretly recorded the last meeting you had with him."

The older man looked askance at his PA.

"Seems like that recording might send you up the river," Becky continued, "and I've got it."

He studied her for a moment. "For the sake of argument, let's pretend such a recording does exist…what do you want for it?"

Becky shook her head. "No, I'm not going to give it to you—ever. It's currently locked up someplace safe. If you want it to stay that way—out of the hands of the authorities—then you need to forget all about my friends and family."

The man smiled. "You have my word."

"I'm not talking about a promise," Becky said. "I need you to know that I have it. I need you to be aware that I'm going to make many copies and keep them in many safety deposit boxes in many different banks. I need you to understand that if anything ever happens to me, there will be clear instructions in my will for those recordings to be sent to any and all interested parties."

The man frowned. "I do understand…but you need to understand something as well. If I hear so much as a whisper that this recording you say exists is being used as evidence against me, then—"

"You won't," Becky interrupted. "So long as the people I love remain safe, no one's ever going to listen to that recording…not even after the feds convict you with all the evidence they've already compiled."

The man smiled again, though diffidently this time. "Fair enough, Mrs. Payley—that's fair enough."

Chapter 56

The Faculty Lounge bartender slid a fresh pitcher of beer across the bar to Weston. "Quite a crowd in here tonight."

The bartender nodded. "These end of the semester blowouts tend to get a little out of hand. Wouldn't be surprised if half these professors can't spell Ph.D. by the end of the night."

"That's okay—he works for a police department and can't spell PD." Weston turned to Slim and refilled his empty glass.

Slim sipped at the beer foam. "You know, all the saloons I've gone to in my life, I ain't never been to a college bar before…rowdier than I imagined."

"Are the mayor and chief still planning to stop by tonight?"

"I doubt it. They got an anonymous tip on the whereabouts of that missing maypole this afternoon." Slim shrugged. "We've been seeing a lot of them lately…thought it might be nice to take a night off."

Edwin sidled up to the bar. "I've a nearly empty glass as well."

"And as fate would have it, I've a nearly full pitcher." Weston doled out more beer.

Edwin spotted Vance approaching the bar through a crowd of tweed. "Are you old enough to be in here, young man?"

"I'm old enough to be here," Vance replied, "but not old enough to buy a drink."

"Well, rules are rules, but let me find you a glass, and I'll pour you a free beer," offered Weston.

"No thanks, I'm good," said Vance. "I just stopped by to say 'hey.' Now that my finals are finally over, I'd like to catch up with a few of my friends before they leave campus for the summer."

"These wouldn't happen to be girlfriends, would they Vancy?" asked Becky.

Vance spun around to see his mother and Kate standing behind him. "Mom, where did you come from?"

"According to my research," said Kate, "when it comes to their sons, mothers can appear from almost anywhere."

"I think it's going to be a long summer at home, Van." Weston turned to Kate. "It sounds like you've been studying up on motherhood...and I noticed that you're not drinking."

Kate grinned coyly. "We're here to fete H.P. tonight...not to engage in wild speculation and inuendo."

After taking a long drink, Edwin held out his empty beer glass again. "I'm all for feting, but I'm still not sure what this fete is for. Is it supposed to be H.P.'s retirement party, or are we celebrating that he'll back in his teaching position come the fall? Is this a farewell to his Pirate Hunter series, or are we hailing the character's forthcoming return?"

"Knowing how indecisive H.P. has been over the years about big life decisions, I'm sure he has any dumber of ideas." Weston replenished Edwin's glass. "So if you're drinking for two, does that mean Kate is eating for two?"

"Where is the man of the hour, anyway?" asked Kate.

Slim pointed to the pool table across the barroom. "I see him over there. Van, want to shoot a game before you go meet up with your buddies? With my busted wing, you've got a fair to middling chance of winning."

"Sure," Vance answered. "There's a table in the residence hall that I've been practicing on...when I take a break from my studies that is, which is rarely, of course."

Becky rolled her eyes. "Nice save, kid."

Edwin followed the pair. "I believe I'll join you two. I've always appreciated the aesthetics of the game—akin to a colorful orrery."

Kate grabbed her husband's hand. "I think I'll tag along too so that Weston can't interrogate me further about my teetotaling."

Weston put his arm around his wife. "Finally...I thought we'd never get rid of them—just you and me out on the town."

"We should enjoy it while we can...I get the sense that our days of Kim being available to watch the kids are numbered."

"She's got a new catch on the line, huh?"

"She won't admit it...but I know my sister. I'd say she's got her hook set pretty deep."

Weston shook his head. "Poor fish."

"Speaking of budding romances, where's Vicky tonight?"

"H.P. mentioned yesterday that after filing her story, she left town for another assignment...and is back with her on-again-off-again girlfriend. Apparently that particular bud of a romance has been nipped."

Becky raised her eyebrows. "I liked her, but honestly I never saw them as a good match. Still, it's a shame that H.P. doesn't have a special someone to share his special night with."

"Don't go feeling too sorry for him. Maybe he'll meet somebody here...speak of the devil, and he shall appear."

H.P. set his empty beer glass on the bar.

Weston refilled his glass. "A foursome just went over to shoot pool with you."

"I know, but I surrendered the table so that they could play doubles instead."

"That was nice of you," said Becky.

"Not really, I just won after my last opponent scratched on the eight ball, and I so rarely win that I thought it wise to rest on my laurels. From what I heard, you deserve a laurel wreath yourself for your convincing performance, pretending your partner was dead...sounds like something out of one of my Pirate Hunter stories."

"Where do you think I got the idea?" asked Becky.

"How could you," Weston grouched. "You haven't even read all my Spinster books yet."

"There are so many of them, and I want to savor each one over time...a long, long time." Becky refilled her beer glass, leaving Weston with an empty pitcher once more. "I'm gonna go watch them play pool and try to determine just how rare Vancy's study breaks are by how much his game has improved."

Weston looked at the empty pitcher and then his own empty glass. "How do you like that? I just ordered this pitcher and didn't get a single drop of beer for myself."

H.P. sipped his beer. "Everyone always says that you're nothing if not selfless...no, my mistake—selfish is what they always say."

Weston gestured to the bartender for another pitcher. "Too bad Vicky couldn't stick around—should be a fun night."

"This isn't her scene," replied H.P. "Trust me, I know...we came here several times when we were together."

"Maybe you bringing her to places like this is what turned her into a lesbian."

"No, she had those proclivities long before I met her."

"I suppose her attraction to you makes some sense since you've got a strong lesbian aura about you...in a good way."

H.P. sighed. "And you've got a strong jackass aura about you...in a bad way."

Weston noticed a familiar face entering the bar. "Your words cut me to the quick...especially in light of all I've done for you lately."

H.P. chuckled. "And what have you done for me lately?"

The bartender slid a new pitcher of beer to Weston. "Another glass as well, please—tout de suite, barkeep."

"Who's the glass for?" asked H.P.

Weston filled the empty glass the bartender set on the bar and then his own. "I'd like to direct your attention to door number one."

H.P. glanced over toward the front door and then, doing a double take, looked again. He waved at Lauren Ipsum. "What did you do?"

"What needed doing." Weston took up his beer glass

in one hand and the pitcher in the other, leaving the new glass waiting in his spot at the bar. "I am a romance writer, after all…and just like a late-night massage artist, I know the importance of a happy ending."

Epilogue

Weston pulled into the gas station, worried the fumes in his car's tank wouldn't be enough to make it to the pump. He hastily exited his sedan and set about the process of refueling.

H.P. peered around the side of the adjacent pump. "You know, when I'm in a hurry, I hold my breath to help slow down time. It doesn't actually work, but it makes me light-headed, and so I don't care as much anymore that I'm running late."

Weston looked up from entering his zip code on the payment keypad. "Hey there, stranger…we didn't see much of you over the summer."

"Yeah, I've been busy…finally finished my book. I'm dedicating it to the Lead family. I found out that my old friend still has a few distant relatives living, so I'm going to give them copies when it's released and let them know how much he meant to me."

"That sounds like a fine idea." Weston peeked over the top of the pump and noticed a late model coupe. "I see you got yourself a new set of wheels."

"Well, they're new to me. I've also been traveling quite a bit this summer."

"Down south, I imagine."

H.P. nodded. "Yes, I've been seeing a good deal of Lauren these past few months."

"If it's really been a good deal, then I bet you're

seeing all of her."

"One day I hope your adolescent brain catches up to your old-man hair." H.P. took note of Weston's hybrid. "You got a new car too…surprised you opted for something so technology forward."

"Right, I have to fill this one with both gas and electricity, which Becca somehow convinced me is a good thing. Van's been driving this car more than I have lately; I just noticed he didn't plug it in last night and, of course, left the tank on empty. We're taking him back to school today. I'm driving over to Kim's before Slim leaves for work to swap him for his truck, so we can pack up the boy's gear…not sure how he's going to fit it all into his dorm room, but he's a big-time sophomore now, so he thinks he's got it all figured out. Judging by all the stuff you've got packed in your car, maybe you should've asked to borrow Slim's pickup too. Will Van be seeing you around campus this semester?"

The nozzle in H.P.'s coupe clicked; he removed it, replacing it on the pump. "No, Lauren's community college had an opening for a writing instructor, so I'm extending my so-called sabbatical with the university again."

"You think you'll ever go back?"

"I haven't made up my mind yet. I'll see how it goes down there. What you did a few years ago—moving to a small town, making a fresh start—it suits you…you've found your place. I'd like to find mine too."

"You could always move here and commute to campus. As you know, our gas is cheaper, and we're right on the interstate."

H.P. looked toward the on-ramp a quarter mile up the road. "Nah, this town isn't big enough for the both of us."

Weston watched as his friend got into the car. "See you around, nimrod."

H.P. rolled down his window as he drove away. "Not if I see you first."

A word about the author…

Wesley Payton has a B.A. in Rhetoric/Philosophy and an M.A. in English. He has been a short-story presenter for the Illinois Philological Association. His play *Way Station* was selected for a Next Draft reading in 2015, and *What Does a Question Weigh?* was selected for a staged reading as part of the 2017 Chicago New Work Festival. He is the author of the novels *Lead Tears, Darkling Spinster, Darkling Spinster No More, Standing in Doorways, Raison Deidre, Oblong, Intimate Recreation, Downstate Illinois, The House Painter and the Pirate Hunter, Immurdered: Some Time to Kill, Dissimiles: More's the Pity,* and *Namastab: Transition into Decompose.*

Wesley and his family live in Oak Park, Illinois. Find out more about the author and his books here: http://wespayton.weebly.com/